# Sleigh Bells & Second Chances

A Frosty Season Series

Katie Winters

# Chapter One

Just two hours from the Canadian border, the sleepy town of Wilmington, New York, was tucked between the lush, sweeping green of the Adirondack Mountains, a few miles away from the frothing beauty of Flume Falls and flanked by the glinting Ausable River. It was often only a stop-over for those yearning for the escapism of the mountain range, long days of fishing and hiking, and fresh air.

But Trudy, who hadn't lived in Wilmington for nearly thirty years, saw Wilmington as an emotional trap. After the five-hour drive from Boston, she walked along the river, her cheeks pink and frozen with tears and her head thudding with sorrow. She watched as a grizzly-haired man on the opposite riverbed swung his fishing line happily, unaffected by winter. It was only three weeks till Christmas, and Trudy had to steel herself for what was to come next. She needed strength for the holiday season; she needed Christmas magic. But right now, broken-hearted on the banks of the Ausable, she wasn't sure how to get back into her Chevy, start the engine, and drive the rest of the way to the Hollow's Grove Inn. She'd never felt so depleted.

It had all begun two days ago. She'd been in the back office of The Lucky Bean, the coffee franchise she owned and operated in a city nicknamed Beantown, going over spreadsheets, making notes, and avoiding the clock on her computer – the one that told her that three hours ago, it had been time to go home. In front, two coffee shop employees finished up for the day, grinding the last coffee beans for college students who were cramming for finals.

Trudy's phone had rung with a Wilmington area code — a different number from her aunt's, the only person who ever contacted her from this neck of the woods. Her heart had immediately stopped beating. Somehow, within the belly of her soul, she'd just known.

"She died peacefully in her sleep," Aunt Olivia's lawyer had said over the phone. "It was a brief illness."

Trudy hadn't known what to do. Her Aunt Olivia hadn't even been seventy years old yet, far too young to succumb to a brief illness. She'd stuttered with nonsensical questions, wanting to say something that would make the lawyer change his mind or tell her there'd been some kind of mistake.

Instead, he'd told her, "Your aunt passed on her inn to you."

Trudy had stood up in her chair with surprise. "Pardon me?"

"The Hollow's Grove Inn? I assume you know your Aunt Olivia has owned and operated the inn for the past ten years."

Trudy had known. She and her husband had visited the inn briefly about eight years ago, sleeping in what Aunt Olivia had called "the guest room of honor" and inhaling their weight in local cuisine before returning to Boston. Aunt Olivia had taken her hands in hers and whispered, "Don't be a stranger." But Trudy had allowed so much time to pass between visits. And she'd hardly ever picked up the phone to call.

Although Trudy was heavy with responsibilities in Boston, she managed to take several weeks off from her franchise to drive up to Wilmington. Her plan was to get through the funeral, finish out the holiday season of the inn, and promptly sell it. An adorable, upstate inn like that was assuredly somebody's dream. It wasn't hers.

No. She was already living out her dreams in Boston. She'd worked tirelessly to get herself out of her childhood circumstances, to build her career, and to escape who she'd once been. Wilmington couldn't drag her back down again, no matter how heavy with nostalgia she currently felt.

Trudy forced herself back to her vehicle, which she'd parked on Main Street beneath a twinkling array of lights strung over the street. Every tree had been decorated for the holidays, with hardly a branch without tinsel or cheer. A downtown bakery had decorated their front windows with Sugar Plum Fairies from *The Nutcracker*; the bank had painted a snowy sledding scene on their window; and the courthouse featured a Nativity Scene, baby Jesus swaddled in soft blankets, Joseph and Mary gazing down upon him. As Trudy emotionally prepared herself for the drive ahead, only three cars went down the road— proof she was miles away from city life. Wilmington was slow. Its two thousand residents preferred it that way.

The Hollow's Grove Inn was three blocks away, nestled beneath the reaching arms of ancient oaks and maples, all of which had lost their leaves for winter. Every bit of the Victorian home sizzled with character, with its decorative eaves, wrap-around porch, pointed red rooftops, and second-story terrace. Trudy parked in front of it and exhaled all the air from her lungs, remembering her and her husband out on the front porch, sharing a pitcher of iced tea with Aunt Olivia as the leaves flickered shadows across their faces. How she'd loved both of them!

Trudy entered the inn and checked herself in the mirror in the foyer, drawing her brunette waves behind her ears and opening her eyes wider, trying to pump herself up.

"Welcome to the Hollow's Grove!" A woman's voice rang out from the front desk.

Trudy turned to find a woman in her mid-sixties, with white curly hair, Coke bottle glasses, and a shepherd's wool sweater with Santa embroidered in the center. She wasn't even five feet tall and could barely peer over the counter.

"Hi," Trudy said hesitantly, drawing closer. "My name is Trudy. Trudy Potter. My aunt was Olivia."

Both of the woman's hands flew to her mouth as she gasped and hurried around the counter. "You poor dear!" She threw her arms around Trudy and cradled her. Absently, Trudy remembered this was one of the first hugs she'd been given in months.

"My name is Frankie," the woman told her, withdrawing her arms. "I've worked part-time here at the Hollow's Inn for the past five years. Odds and ends, you know. Whatever Olivia needed help with."

"It's a pleasure to meet you." Trudy tried to smile.

"I was devastated to hear about Olivia," Frankie said. "I never saw it coming. One day, she had a light cough, and the next..." She hesitated. "She wasn't much older than me, you know. And I think, well." She paused again. "I might have been her closest friend. And I sometimes feel I didn't know her at all."

Trudy frowned, caught off-guard. The Olivia she'd known thirty years ago had been tremendously charming, quick with a joke or a laugh, and always eager to invite people to her home for wine, food, and conversation. Back then, Trudy had been a dark and depressive teenager, and Olivia's optimism hadn't ever penetrated her thick walls.

Trudy explained she was here to help with the holiday season, but she didn't disclose that she planned to sell the inn afterward. Frankie's shoulders loosened.

"This is one of our busiest times," she said. "I thought I was going to fall apart with all the responsibilities."

"I own a coffee franchise down in Boston," Trudy explained. "I'm used to chaos."

"That'll serve you well here," Frankie joked, reaching out to sweep a dead leaf from Trudy's winter coat. "I'll show you the ropes, shall I? After that, I need to go to a doctor's appointment! These knees aren't what they used to be. And boy, have I run myself ragged since Olivia got sick." Frankie touched her chest, her face falling. "God rest her soul."

Trudy did her best to listen closely to everything Frankie told her— how to manage the books, how they kept tabs on who stayed in which rooms, and the names of all the kitchen staff, waitstaff, maids, and handymen. When Trudy asked why they didn't use a computer to handle logistics, Frankie led her to the back office to show off their thirty-year-old computer, which hadn't turned on since 2017. "Olivia kept saying she wanted to get it fixed," Frankie explained sadly. "But since then, pen and paper have worked all right for us."

There was something remarkably sad about that old, boxy computer in the corner. It didn't even have a layer of dust on it, as though Aunt Olivia or the maids had continued to clean it, putting their hope in its future. If Trudy had had any plans whatsoever to keep the inn in her own name, she would have taken that thing to the dump immediately and started over.

But it wasn't her job to rejuvenate the place. She just had to keep it afloat until January 1. After that, she promised herself she could go on vacation somewhere—Hawaii or Bermuda or Bali, somewhere with turquoise water, where she could drink juice from a coconut and promptly fall asleep. This harsh winter would be nothing but a memory.

# Chapter Two

Not ten minutes after Frankie left for the day, a toddler burst from the staircase on a mad dash away from his mother. His mother wore only one of the lavender robes the inn gave its guests, and her hair was wet and wild behind her. She was calling for her son, who seemed to think this was the best way to spend an afternoon. Just as the toddler tore across the foyer and into the adjoined dining room, an older woman with a rocky gait walked to her table for lunch and nearly fell. Her cries echoed through the little space, terrifying the toddler so much that he stopped long enough for his mother to scoop him up.

Trudy bolted into the dining room to make sure the older woman was all right. Her cheeks were pale, and she shivered as she sat down. One of the waiters, a twenty-something guy with black hair, appeared a second later with her coffee, stricken.

"Glinda, are you all right?"

"He came out of nowhere." Glinda tried to lift up the mug of coffee but put it down a second later, exhausted.

"I'm terribly sorry," the mother gushed, her cheeks red with embarrassment. "He always wants to run away."

Glinda hardly glanced her way as though the idea of accepting the apology was too much for her.

"You know," Glinda continued, "My husband and I have been coming to the Hollow's Grove Inn during the Christmas season for the past forty-five years? And I've never seen it such a mess. The list of things that have gone wrong since my arrival is a mile long."

The waiter winced and glanced up at Trudy for help. Trudy tried to drum up all her available hospitality skills.

"Glinda, I'm really sorry about that," Trudy said. "Can we accommodate you in any way right now?"

"We?" Glinda sniffed at her. "Who are you?"

"I'm temporarily in charge of the inn," Trudy said.

"Temporarily?" Glinda demanded as the waiter slunk back, hiding himself in the kitchen.

"My Aunt Olivia owned the inn the previous ten years," Trudy explained timidly. "But she just passed away a few days ago. Obviously, the inn is reeling without her. I hope you can be a little patient with us during this difficult time."

But Glinda was an ornery woman, looking to find fault in anyone and anything. "This inn has been through plenty of owners in the past. I've never noticed such a drop in quality. I mean, look around!" She gestured toward the dining room walls, which were adorned with paintings of the Adirondack Mountains from long-gone eras. "Not a single Christmas tree. Not a single hanging light! You advertise yourself as a Christmas destination, but you don't deliver! If my husband were here, he would demand his money back."

Trudy's heart ached with the sudden realization: the

woman was alone. Her husband wasn't there. Probably, he'd died.

They had that in common, Trudy thought. They were both widows, up against the cruelty of the world, feeling so alone.

Trudy tried to be honest with Glinda— and stroke her ego just a bit. "I just arrived to handle all things Christmas here at the inn. The staff is trying to show me the ropes, but I might need help from someone like you. Someone with so many wonderful memories here at the inn."

But Glinda had fallen deeper within herself. Her cheeks were pale, and she muttered into her coffee, picking the inn apart. A moment later, the waiter arrived with her stew, fresh rolls, and a big glass of water, and he took Trudy's elbow, leading her back into the foyer.

"She's a very angry person," he explained softly. "But she's been through a lot."

Trudy nodded and crossed her arms. "I've only been here fifteen minutes, and I already feel like I'm doing a terrible job."

"It's going to be fine," the waiter said. "It's supposed to snow soon, which is always a welcome distraction for annoying guests." He laughed, then added, "Usually, our guests are very kind and excited to be here. Glinda just needs a little TLC."

"Thank you for being there for her," Trudy said.

"I'm Max," the waiter said, extending his hand. "I think I was upstairs when you were introduced to the others." He paused. "I was sorry to hear about Olivia. I didn't know her well, but I worked with her for the past four years. She was the heart and soul of this place."

As Max turned to retreat back to the dining room,

Trudy's heart thudded, and she asked, "Why do you feel you didn't know her well? If you worked side-by-side for four years, I mean."

Max considered this. "Olivia kept to herself. She preferred it that way." He pressed his tongue to his top lip, considering. "She came alive during Christmas, though."

Trudy winced. "I'll start the decorating process as soon as I can."

"She'd like that," Max said.

But before Trudy could ask someone where they kept the Christmas decorations, she had to put out three more guest "fires"— one involving a fifty-year-old man's apparent misplacement of the large iron key required for his room. According to Frankie, they only had two keys for each of the rooms, and it was very expensive to replace them. It had begun to occur to Olivia just how little the coffee industry had prepared her for the stress of operating an inn. At The Lucky Bean, people came in, ordered coffee, drank it, and then they left. They never put any undue needs upon her. They didn't lean on her to make their holiday dreams come true.

In fact, her anxiety mounted to such a degree that she'd begun to think something really was wrong back in Boston. Around seven, she took a break on the front porch, inhaling sharply cold air, and called one of her store managers.

"Monica? Hey. How is everything?" Trudy's voice wavered.

"Hey, girl! It's great. We've had insane revenue the past few hours. You know how people love to sit in the coffee shop and watch the snow fall."

Trudy's heart thumped. It seemed incredible that

eight thousand things had gone wrong at the Hollow's Grove while her baby down in Boston just kept swimming.

"How are things in Wilmington?" Monica asked.

"Oh? Um. Weird," Trudy said with a laugh. "I'm already looking forward to coming home."

"It sounds so magical there," Monica breathed. "A quaint, snow-capped village in upstate New York? I would kill to be there today and not dirty old Boston."

Monica was probably the closest thing Trudy had to a best friend these days, but that didn't mean Trudy had shared many details of her past with Monica — nor the very strange relationship she'd once had with her Aunt Olivia. Now that her husband was gone, she was pretty sure nobody knew, for example, that Aunt Olivia had taken Trudy in at the age of sixteen when nobody else wanted her. When Trudy had refused to go to public school, Olivia had agreed to homeschool her— and when she'd resisted that, Olivia had bought her books to study for the GED and driven her to the test center. She'd allowed Trudy to do everything on her terms. Until Trudy had up and left for Boston, bent on leaving her old life in the rearview.

Out on the street in front of the inn, a large truck pulled an even larger trailer behind it, upon which were stacks of Christmas trees. To Trudy's surprise, the truck stopped in front of the inn, and the man inside it stopped the engine, jumped out, and headed toward the Hollow's Grove. Like Trudy, the man was in his late forties, with thick black-and-gray hair, a black beard fit for a lumberjack, a broad chest, and thick, muscular arms. He wore a Carhartt coat and a pair of tan gloves, and his blue eyes matched the sharp blue of the sky above.

"I have to call you back," Trudy said to Monica.

"You don't have to do that," Monica said. "Remember. I got this. You have too much on your plate as it is."

Trudy thanked Monica again and hung up just as the lumberjack man breezed past her toward the front door.

"Excuse me?"

The man stalled at the door and glanced toward her, wearing a soft smile. "Good evening!"

"Um. Hi! What are you doing?" Trudy asked.

The man gestured toward the trailer. "I'm here to drop off all those trees. It's December 1st! Time to decorate this old place, don't you think?"

Trudy's voice was high-pitched. "Wait. Did Olivia order all of those trees?" There had to be at least twenty-five of them, stacked up on top of one another, tied up with thick tan rope, waiting to unfurl their limbs.

The man's eyes grew shadowed. "I'm sorry. I assumed you were a guest here. You know Olivia?"

"She was my aunt."

"Was?" The man paused as he removed his gloves, stitching his black eyebrows, thick as caterpillars, together. "What do you mean?"

"She died two days ago." Trudy scrunched up her hand and dug her fingernails into her palm. Oh, how she hated death. It seemed to follow her around, to lurk around every corner. It was beginning to feel personal.

The man touched the back of his neck. All the inertia he'd brought with him from the truck fell apart in an instant. "Gosh. The last time I talked to her, she had that cough. But I never imagined..." He trailed off.

"It was very sudden. I don't know what to make of it, either."

"I imagine not. I'm just so sorry for your loss." After a

heavy silence, the man stepped forward and unfurled his hand to shake hers. "My name is Jack Carter. I own the Christmas tree farm between Wilmington and Burks Falls."

Trudy nodded, as though she'd passed the Christmas tree farm hundreds of times. "Trudy."

The feel of his large hand over hers made Trudy breathe deeper. "I just had a guest complaining that we hadn't decorated properly for Christmas."

Jack nodded toward the trees. "Olivia was always one of my best clients. She used to come out and hand-select the trees herself, but she recently told me she trusted me enough to make the selection myself. I'm embarrassed to say how proud that made me. At the age of nearly fifty, your Aunt Olivia finally recognized me as worthy."

Trudy laughed gently, her eyes filling with the first tears she'd allowed herself since her arrival.

Jack looked stricken, and he stuttered for a second, searching for words. "I'll get some of your staff members to help me set up the trees."

"That would be amazing," Trudy said.

"I take it you're handling the inn for your aunt?"

Trudy nodded, again holding herself back from saying that it was just until January.

"That's very kind of you," Jack offered. "This old place meant so much to her. It was just about the only thing she cared about in the world till the end."

Trudy pressed the sleeve of her coat against her cheek, catching her tears. "I'm beginning to think she was a loner the past few years."

She didn't add what she was thinking: that Trudy, too, had been a loner, that she understood what it meant to throw yourself so completely into your work so that you could pretend your life was filled with meaning.

Jack hesitated before he opened the door to fetch some of the stronger-bodied men in the inn to help. "Olivia lit up around Christmas," he said, echoing what Max had said earlier. "And I know her heart would be glad to see you here."

Just as soon as Jack disappeared, someone rang the bell at the front desk, demanding Trudy back inside for another bit of drama. As she hurried back into the comforting warmth, she heard her aunt's voice in her head— so nourishing and kind. She willed herself to be just like her, if only for a while. Just to uphold the spirit of the beautiful place until the year was through.

# Chapter Three

The funeral for Olivia Wilson was held two days after Trudy's arrival in Wilmington. Although Olivia had often been too busy with the inn to attend, she'd been a member of the Wilmington First Presbyterian Church, and she'd requested that her funeral be held there. Trudy arrived thirty minutes before it was set to begin and sat primly in the second row, waiting, jittery with nerves. Olivia hadn't wanted an open casket, but the casket itself was on display in the front of the church, piled high with autumn flowers.

Trudy couldn't help but remember the last time she'd been to a funeral. Five years ago, her husband, Ben, had died of cancer. Twice over the span of three years, they'd thought they'd beaten it, but cancer had always crept back into his body again. It had robbed Trudy and Ben of the life they'd promised each other— vacations and hobbies and long nights talking over wine. Because Ben had also had cancer as a teenager, he hadn't been able to have children, and Trudy had welcomed this, deciding she wanted nothing more than to spend her life at Ben's side. They hadn't needed anyone else.

Oh, goodness. It was terrible to think of Ben now at Aunt Olivia's funeral. It nearly brought Trudy to her knees.

Aunt Olivia's funeral was not well-attended. About fifteen people filtered into the church, clutching their bulletins. Reverend Miller stood at the front of the church, adjusting his horn-rimmed spectacles, his gown silky and catching the light. It broke Trudy's heart, remembering what Jack, Max, and Frankie had told her. Olivia hadn't had a real community. Frankie might have gone to the funeral, but Trudy had needed her to handle the front desk.

The funeral was brief. Reverend Miller said kind words about Aunt Olivia, about her work in the community, her love of Christmas, and her loyalty to her niece, Trudy. Trudy had called him ahead of time, asking him to work this into his speech. She'd wanted people to know that Olivia had been her only real guardian during her teenage years and that she would have wound up on the streets if it hadn't been for her. How she wished she could go back and tell her teenage self to be more grateful for what Aunt Olivia was giving her.

But Trudy had been broken. She'd been raised on processed foods, Ramen noodles, chalky candy, and boxes of generic macaroni and cheese. Her mother had been an alcoholic, and she'd often left her home alone to fend for herself. When Trudy had landed in Wilmington, Olivia had tried to hug her, but Trudy had rejected it. The first act of goodwill Trudy had allowed Olivia, if she remembered correctly, was the dentist trip. Yes, she'd had seven cavities— but gosh, she'd felt better after that.

It had been the first step forward, all because of Aunt Olivia.

* * *

Trudy had requested that the church bulletin include an invitation to come back to the Hollow's Grove Inn for a post-funeral meal. She supposed, now, she shouldn't have been surprised to see so few people milling into the inn for the occasion, removing their scarves slowly, glancing at one another as though suspicious of anyone else who'd arrived. A long table had been set, heavy with roasted chicken, rolls, mashed potatoes, gravy, and stuffing, and only about eight people from the service sat at a couple of dining room tables, sipping water and tea.

Just before Trudy stood to thank everyone for coming, a blonde woman in her forties appeared in the doorway. She wore a powder blue peacoat and a thick white hat, and she looked fidgety and strange, rubbing her palms together as she approached the small wake. Trudy hadn't seen her at the funeral. Perhaps because she was the only person there around her age – and out of curiosity, Trudy intercepted her, forcing a smile.

"Hi. Thank you for coming. I'm Trudy."

Trudy now stood between the woman and the tables, blocking her path.

"Hello. I'm Emily." The woman raised her hand and slipped it into Trudy's to shake. It was surprisingly frigid. "I was sorry to hear about your aunt. I tried to get over to Wilmington in time for the service, but I got held up at work."

"You're here now," Trudy said. "Where are you coming from?"

"The next town over. Burks Falls."

Trudy remembered Jack's Christmas tree farm, located between Wilmington and Burks Falls. Why hadn't Jack made it to the service, anyway?

"And how did you know my aunt?" Trudy asked.

Emily looked flustered, as though the question was much more complicated than it seemed on the surface. "Gosh. She was a family friend, I guess. Maybe more like family, for a while. But that was all a long time ago. Things change all at once, sometimes."

In the dining room, a few of the inn's waitstaff had begun to pass out ice waters, speaking in soft and sensitive voices as they asked for further drink orders. Trudy glanced back to ensure everyone was situated, then returned her attention to Emily, whose face was drawn. As she glanced around her, taking stock of the Christmas trees, as yet undecorated, the ornate grandfather clock in the corner that swung its pendulum, and the oil paintings of the mountains, she looked as though she dropped into another world, far from this one.

"Would you like to sit down?" Trudy asked, breaking her reverie.

Emily blinked quickly, forcing her eyes back to Trudy's. "I really can't stay."

Trudy wondered why. Was it the inn? Was it filled with ghosts?

"I'm sorry to hear that. Is there anything I can do to make it more comfortable here for you?" Trudy asked.

Emily tucked a blonde curl behind her ear, and her eyes glistened with tears. "You don't have to do a thing. This place is comfortable already." She stuttered. "It's so beloved."

Trudy's head throbbed with confusion. She sensed an

enormous history behind Emily's words. Did Emily know why her aunt had become such a recluse? Why so few people had attended her service?

"Emily, before you go," Trudy began, smoothing her dress over her stomach, "I wondered if you could help me."

Emily's eyebrows crept together.

"It's just that, back when I lived with my aunt as a teenager, she was an important part of this community," Trudy spoke in a low voice. "She was always out and about. Her social calendar was difficult for me, as a very lonely teenager, to comprehend. But now..." She trailed off and tilted her head toward the eight people seated in the dining room. "I don't know. I've heard from a few people that she kept to herself over the past decade or so. Do you happen to know why?"

Emily wet her lips nervously, suddenly looking much younger than her forty-something years. "Time had its way with Olivia," she said softly. "She had a very rough time."

This was perhaps the vaguest thing Emily could have said. Trudy sputtered with disbelief, searching for another angle to get to the bottom of this.

Before she could, Emily added, "I just hate that there won't be a Festival of Frost Floats this year." She swallowed and tugged at the fingers of her thick gloves.

"What do you mean?"

"Your Aunt Olivia was in charge," Emily explained. "Everyone knew it was time for Christmas when she darkened their business doors to organize everything. It was usually the only time I saw her out and about, wearing a little Christmas sweater and asking people to decorate floats. Gosh, that should have been my first sign there was something wrong. She usually starts preparing before Thanksgiving, for goodness' sake." Emily's eyes darkened as though she blamed herself for being unable to save Olivia.

"Isn't there something we can do?" Trudy asked.

Emily looked distracted, glancing back toward the foyer. "I don't know. Probably not, right? It's three weeks till Christmas, and I'm sure you have enough on your plate handling this inn."

Trudy stared for a long time at the nearest Christmas tree from Jack's farm, its thick branches shimmering with health, its stump stuck in a watered tree stand. Where were the Christmas decorations? In the attic? The basement? The back shed? Why was it she felt she'd worked tirelessly since her arrival from Boston, only to remain five steps behind at every juncture? It would be a miracle if she got through this wake, let alone the Christmas season.

"I have to run," Emily admitted, touching Trudy's arm as she moved away from her. "But I'm really glad I got to meet you, Trudy. Your aunt was a wonderful woman. And I'm sorry to see her go."

Trudy was too anxious to eat. She wandered through the dining room tables, thanking her guests quietly for coming together at the inn, listening to their few tales about Olivia. One older woman spoke about Olivia's Frost Float from last year, upon which she'd created a remarkable winter scene inspired by *The Wizard of Oz*.

"She dressed like Dorothy," she explained excitedly, "and a few of the other inn employees were the other characters, you know. The Scarecrow, the Lion, and the Tinman."

"Don't forget the wicked witch!" a man added from down the table, his fork flashing over a mound of stuffing.

"And she filled the float with fake snow," the woman continued, "and played music from a speaker system! I remember asking her, 'Olivia, how on earth do you get that new-fangled thing to play?' And she laughed and told me she spent hours watching a YouTube tutorial. Can you believe that? That she didn't bother to get help? Oh, but your Aunt Olivia was like that. I imagine, even if she'd been sick a much longer time, she never would have called anyone for help. She was too proud."

By five, everyone cleared out of the Hollow's Grove Inn, touching Trudy's hand gently and stepping out into the whipping winds. Trudy remained alone in the dining room, staring down at large metal trays filled with left-overs. In the kitchen, the staff was already preparing for the inn's traditional dinner— a selection of salmon, pork, chicken, beef, and pasta dishes. Nobody at the inn wanted to eat food from the wake.

After reading online about a local food bank, Trudy called to ask if they had the bandwidth for so much food.

"We have a call sheet for families in need," the woman on the other line assured her. "They're always eager for a warm, nourishing meal."

Trudy worked diligently, sliding the metal tops over the heaps of lukewarm food. Max, who'd arrived to serve dinner, helped her pile the boxes into the trunk, back, and passenger side of her car, his muscles straining at the weight. "You're doing a good thing here, Trudy," he said as he skipped back inside, coatless, his forearms white with cold.

Trudy drove seven minutes to the local food bank, where three employees guided her to park directly by the door. This time, Trudy was required to carry only two boxes as the food bank staff took over, whipping the containers into the massive ovens in the downstairs kitchen and filling the center with smells of butter and sage. Already, families who'd been called to dine began to arrive, removing puffy coats and hanging them in the front closet. Children scampered to the side of the large dining hall, dropping to their knees to investigate one another's toys or books, as their parents milled around behind them, greeting one another nervously. Trudy hoped they weren't too embarrassed about asking for help. She remembered her own mother, her empty bank account, the kitchen cabinets filled with dust and packets of crackers. "We don't take handouts!" she'd screamed at Trudy several times, her hand wrapped tightly around a bottle of booze.

"Trudy!" A familiar voice found Trudy's ears, and Trudy turned to find a fifty-something woman with gray hair and a loose purple dress coming toward her. It was Megan, the woman Trudy had spoken to on the phone, and she took Trudy's hands in hers and said, very quietly, "We can't thank you enough."

"It's my pleasure," Trudy assured her.

Megan guided Trudy to the far corner, where they watched parents corral their children to available seats, drawing their fingers through their hair in an effort to tame it. The food was nearly finished, and staff members had begun to pass out glasses of water, milk, and juice. Trudy had a strange itch to tell Megan she'd come from a world like this, that she'd once been a child who hadn't fully understood why everyone else at school had so much more than her, why they made fun of the way she smelled. Her mother had never taught her to care for herself. She'd never been able to.

"I should get going," Trudy said, touching the neckline of her sweater and watching as a kid of eight or nine scraped his plate clean. She was reminded of a time when she'd been that age, maybe, and sensing she was hungry, her teacher at school had bought her McDonald's. Trudy had thought, at the time, she'd never tasted anything more scrumptious than that burger, its cheese melting cartoonishly over the sides, the pickle a sharp jolt of flavor.

But just then, a young woman in her late twenties, one of the mothers, approached Megan nervously.

"Rina, hello," Megan said kindly. "I hope the meal tastes all right?"

"It's wonderful," Rina said, tugging at her t-shirt, which didn't fit her quite right. She lowered her voice. "I heard a rumor there won't be a toy drive this year?"

Megan's face paled. "We don't have confirmation yet, but it doesn't look like it."

Rina grimaced and glanced back at her children, who tore through rolls, chewing with their mouths open and cackling. "I don't know what I'm going to do. I've been telling them all year that Santa will come if they're good." She paused. "I don't want them to think they haven't been good."

As Megan assured Rina they'd figure something out, somehow, Trudy's heart cracked at the edges. She could see it in Rina's eyes, just how much the world had knocked her down. Rina nodded doubtfully and returned to her table, where she sipped a glass of milk and cleaned her son's cheek of mashed potatoes.

"I've been worried about this ever since I heard about your aunt," Megan whispered.

"What do you mean?"

"Your aunt was in charge of the festival."

"Oh, yes. Frost Floats?" She'd been hearing an awful lot about that tonight.

"The funds she raised through the festival all went toward a Christmas toy drive here at the community center," Megan explained. "We raise our own funds throughout the year, of course, but we always count on the influx of cash from Olivia's festival. I don't know what we'll do."

Trudy was quiet for a long time, listening as Megan spoke with several staff members, giving instructions for clean-up. Three women breezed through the tables, collecting empty plates and refilling glasses of water. The dining hall hummed with post-dinner conversation, lazy yet contented. Trudy wavered from foot to foot, her consciousness fuzzy at the edges. She'd hardly nibbled on anything at the wake.

"It's getting late. You should get home," Megan assured her. "We'll bring the food containers to the inn tomorrow."

Trudy thanked her, walked slowly toward the closet, and donned her coat, listening to the blissful sound of children's laughter. It was a marvel to her that her Aunt Olivia had carried the weight of so many children's Christmases on her shoulders. Why, then, had she died so alone?

# Chapter Four

Trudy parked in the garage around the back of the inn, directly next to her Aunt Olivia's old sedan— another item Trudy would have to figure out what to do with. She made a mental note to call Megan at the community center and ask about donating the car. Surely, one of the families would need it.

In the backyard of the Hollow's Grove Inn, Trudy leaned against the garage wall, inhaling the sharp air, which was spiced from the line of pine trees along the garden wall and thick with the smell of autumn earth beneath the melted snow. The meteorologist projected seven inches by tomorrow, and already, thick and dark clouds rolled above, spitting the occasional snowflake in preparation. Across the back of the inn, orange light filled each of the windows, many of which had curtains drawn before them. Trudy imagined all eight of the rooms, filled with laughter and conversation, her guests sore from long wintry hikes in the mountains or just long strolls through downtown, stopping for food whenever they pleased. How many times had Aunt Olivia stood out in the backyard and watched her inn go to sleep at night? It was a calming feeling.

Trudy entered the inn through the side and breezed past the front desk, where Frankie remained half-chipper, her eyes drooping, but her smile crystallized. Trudy told Frankie to run home— that she could take it from here.

"I could hug you," Frankie said. "My husband made his famous lasagna tonight, and I've been craving it all night long."

As Frankie opened the front door to depart, she bucked back, laughing. "Jack! I didn't see you there. You frightened me."

The Christmas tree farmer held open the door wider, gesturing for Frankie to exit. "Ladies first." His dimples were caverns, and his eyes were illuminated by the porch light.

"You charmer," Frankie teased, hurrying out into the darkness.

Trudy tried to make herself look poised behind the front desk, her chin slightly raised. She remembered, a little too late, that she continued to wear a thick winter hat, which probably looked ridiculous there behind the front desk. Her hair was probably frizzy from the wind; her cheeks were almost assuredly red and chapped.

Jack carried a bouquet of flowers, a mix of chrysanthemums, roses, and orchids, and his eyes were ponderous and meaningful as he approached the desk. Abstractly, Trudy wondered who the flowers were for. Maybe Jack, who wore no wedding ring, had a date after this. Maybe he'd brought more trees for the inn, a last-ditch effort to make the Hollow's Grove even more Christmas-y, perhaps out of guilt.

"Trudy," he said, tugging his own hat from his thick

head of curls. "I'm terribly sorry I missed the service today."

Trudy's lips parted with surprise. Jack strew the bouquet over the front desk, looking sheepish. Were the flowers actually for her? No, she reminded herself. Of course not. They were for Aunt Olivia, in honor of her memory.

"They're beautiful," Trudy managed.

As Jack winced, Trudy couldn't help but think he looked more handsome than ever, his thick eyebrows merging together, his eyes stirring with the density of his emotions. "I tried to get away, but we had an unfortunate incident at the Christmas tree farm. I hope you had an okay turn-out?"

Trudy didn't want to make him feel any worse than he did. "The turn-out was all right," she lied. "I hope everything's okay at the farm?"

"Everyone still has their fingers," Jack said with a sturdy laugh. "Which we couldn't say when the same thing happened five years ago."

"Goodness!" Trudy's eyes bugged out. "I didn't realize you worked in such a dangerous industry."

"Christmas trees are no easy game," Jack assured her. "And I just have a month or so to make as much revenue as I can."

"What do you do when it's not Christmas?"

"All year is Christmas to me," Jack teased, his shoulders loosening. Trudy felt her lips curl into a smile, surprising her. "I have to take care of the trees, of course. But besides that, I'm a woodworker. I make furniture for clients across Burks Falls and Wilmington." His cheeks turned slightly pink as he added, "And last year, I had a big order for a client in New York City."

"You must be really good," Trudy stammered, feeling sheepish.

"I'm just average," Jack insisted, dropping his gaze.

It had been a very long time since Trudy had had so much one-on-one interaction with a man. Since her husband died, she'd kept herself lodged in the back rooms of her coffee shop franchises, hardly peeping her head out to check the weather. Friends had come and gone, attempting to lure her from the cage she'd built for herself yet unable to convince her that the love and sorrow she clung to weren't serving her. Was it possible she'd just needed to get out of Boston? To remember what it meant to exist in another context.

It was ironic. As a teenager, all she'd wanted in the world was to get out of Wilmington, away from her Aunt Olivia. She'd craved the future, knowing it would open up pieces of herself and her personality that she couldn't fully name. But grief, being the monster that it was, had made every bit of her personality gray, soft, meaningless.

"Would you like a cup of cocoa?" Trudy asked.

Trudy asked Jack to man the front desk for a few minutes while she whisked into the private kitchen attached to Aunt Olivia's office, knowing to avoid the staff in the main kitchen during their big post-dinner clean-up. She turned on the water kettle, spooned cocoa mix into two mugs, and waited, her heart simmering with expectation. After she stirred the cocoa, she dropped five mini marshmallows onto the top, watching as the marshmallow sugar shimmered adrift in the brown liquid.

"Did any guests come by?" she asked, approaching Jack from behind.

"Just a few Christmas ghosts," Jack said, taking the mug of cocoa.

Trudy laughed. "What did they say?"

"I don't know if you want to know."

Trudy's blush crawled up her neck and over her cheeks, and she sipped her cocoa, feeling the warm chocolate draw over her tongue and drop down the back of her throat, smooth as velvet, nutty and sweet. Just to make sure, she again checked Jack's left hand to note that he wore no wedding band. Why did she keep doing that? Did she think his flirtation was misguided? Maybe he wasn't flirting at all!

"I hate that I wasn't there for your aunt as much as I should have been the past few years," Jack admitted, his eyes toward the bay window that echoed a beautiful view of the street out front, where snow swept serenely and nestled along the naked limbs of trees.

"It sounds like she didn't want anyone to be there for her," Trudy admitted. "She wanted to be alone."

Jack sighed and palmed the back of his neck. "I don't know if anyone actually wants to be alone. Maybe they tell themselves that, but it's a result of something. They don't want to get hurt again."

"Protection," Trudy agreed, thinking of herself, all alone in Boston, building enormous walls around her heart.

"I was so lost the past few years," Jack said quietly. "Lost in myself and my own emotions. But I should have opened my eyes just a little bit wider if only to care for people like Olivia. That's the reason to live in a small town, isn't it? To be there for one another."

Trudy furrowed her brow, curious. Burly Jack, with his Christmas tree farm and his gorgeous furniture business, didn't seem the type of man who could ever be "lost." It felt as though he hinted toward something enormous, a terrible event that he couldn't fully name. Had he lost his wife the way Trudy had lost her husband? Had he suffered the way she'd suffered?

"I live in the city," Trudy answered quietly. "Maybe because I don't want people checking up on me."

Jack nodded and flashed a soft smile. "Yet the first thing I wanted to do when I got out of work today was come by the inn and make sure you were all right."

Trudy wasn't sure what to say. She filled her mouth with another sip of hot chocolate and returned her gaze to the snow, where flurries intensified into a white wall.

"Okay," Jack interjected. "I think it's finally time I pass on what the Christmas ghosts told me." He raised his eyebrows mysteriously.

"Is this a part of the process of learning to run an inn?" Trudy joked.

"It is." Jack's eyes shimmered with light.

"Then I suppose I have to be ready for their judgment. Bring it on, Christmas ghosts!"

Jack laughed, and his face opened, long crow's feet extending to his hairline. "We just couldn't help but notice you haven't decorated a single one of the Christmas trees. Not a single bauble. Not a single garland. Not even one string of lights!"

Had Jack looked anything but darling, his tone teasing, Trudy might have wilted on the spot. Before she could muster a response, Jack was quick to add: "Lucky for you, Olivia showed me where the decorations are. You want some help?"

With the snow falling torrentially outside and the inn generally quiet, guests nestled in their rooms, Trudy followed Jack to the attic. It was easy for him to pull the string that brought the sturdy wooden ladder down from the ceiling. It was easier still for him to latch the ladder into place and draw himself into the darkness.

"There's a lightbulb up here!" he assured Trudy, peering down at her, his face the only thing she could make out from the hallway below. A second later, she heard the click of the light, and the space was illuminated with white light.

It had been a long time since Trudy had used this much of her upper body strength. Gingerly, she shifted up the ladder and clambered into the attic, coughing twice as her lungs filled with dust.

The attic was nearly as tall as a normal room, with slanted ceilings and a tiny window filled completely with snow. Boxes were piled high on the far wall, labeled with every type of seasonal decoration— Thanksgiving, Halloween, Easter, Christmas, and so on. On the other side of the attic was furniture, spare beds, mattresses, old, ornate desks, and paintings protected with white sheets. Out of curiosity, Trudy pulled one of the sheets back to see a beautiful painting of a New York City street, blurry with rain.

"It's a treasure trove up here," Trudy said.

"Right? You should really go through some of this furniture," Jack suggested. "I bet quite a bit of it is worth something."

Trudy's stomach tied into a knot. She wasn't sure why, but the idea of removing anything from Aunt Olivia's inn made her anxious. Aunt Olivia had held onto all of it for a reason. It wasn't up to Trudy to get rid of it.

Trudy remembered, horribly, that she hadn't gotten rid of any of her husband's belongings back in Boston. His clothes remained in the closet they'd shared. His bike still hung on the wall.

"As you can see," Jack was saying, gesturing like Vana White, "Olivia did not scrimp on Christmas decorations."

It was true. There were twelve boxes of Christmas decorations, divided up between lights, baubles, miniature angels, nativity scenes, wreaths, and a miscellaneous box that contained Christmas-themed teddy bears, Christmas-themed paintings, and a Christmas-themed gnome that Jack was pretty sure normally went out front, on the walkway.

"We have our work cut out for us," Trudy said with a laugh.

"Lights first," Jack suggested. "Everything else we can tackle another day."

Jack's "we" hung in the air between them. Trudy wanted to tell him to take it back; that he shouldn't make promises he couldn't keep.

As Trudy swung one of the light boxes from the shelf, telling her muscles to keep working, something flew out from the back of the wall and wafted slowly to the floor like a dying leaf.

"What was that?" Jack asked.

Trudy placed the box of lights to the side and bent to retrieve a photograph, which had landed face-down. "Maybe it's another message from the Christmas ghosts," she joked as she turned it over.

The photograph featured three women, a man, and a baby seated together on an old, worn-out yellow couch, their eyes alight. Two of the women's mouths were wide open, mid-laughter, and the baby's hair was curly and blonde, dressed up with a white bow. The women had permed hairstyles, high white socks, and tanned, toned legs, and the man wore a bright blue collared shirt, proof of the time period.

"Classic eighties," Jack agreed, bowing his head. "Do you know who they are?"

"I'm pretty sure that's Aunt Olivia," Trudy said, pointing to the woman on the far end of the couch. "She must have been in her twenties here. Gosh, she was gorgeous, wasn't she?"

Aunt Olivia had her arm drawn around the woman to her left, her head bent slightly toward her. It was clear the women knew one another as intimately as sisters. You could feel hundreds of hours of conversations between them. You could feel love beaming off the photograph. Trudy forced her eyes away from Aunt Olivia for a moment to engage with the friend's face beside her— and realized, with a strange jolt in her stomach, that she'd met this woman, too. But where?

"You look white as a sheet," Jack said, reaching out to touch her shoulder. "Let's go downstairs."

Trudy bowed her head.

"It was stupid of me," Jack hurried to add. "You've had such a crazy day. We can decorate the trees another time."

Trudy remained wordless, clinging to the photograph as she climbed down the ladder. Memories swirled in her mind's eye, drawing her deeper into a time she'd forced herself to forget. She felt so caught up in the past, in fact, that after Jack closed the attic and turned to check up on her again, she couldn't remember, for a moment, who he was.

"What can I do for you? More hot chocolate? Tea?" Jack asked. "Come on. Let's get comfortable." His face showed just how much he blamed himself for Trudy's sudden panic. But Jack hadn't placed the photograph between the boxes and the wall. Jack hadn't set up this onslaught of memories. Jack hardly knew anything about Trudy. Maybe Trudy needed to keep it that way.

But a few minutes later, as Trudy sat wrapped in a blanket, watching a fire lick the stones of the fireplace, her hands wrapped around a mug of tea, she found her voice again.

"I'm sorry," she offered.

Jack was squatting by the fireplace, adjusting the logs with a poker. He looked every bit like a burly hero from a romance novel, come to sweep the heroine off her feet. But Trudy, at forty-six, was perhaps the least heroine-like of any woman in the world.

"Why are you sorry?" Jack demanded.

"The photograph just took me out of myself for a little while," Trudy told him. "It felt like being punched in the stomach."

Jack winced and walked toward the couch, where he sat on the opposite end. The firelight traced his perfect features. "Memories can be wicked that way, can't they?"

Trudy nodded and sipped her tea. "Tonight, at the community center, I learned about my Aunt Olivia's work with the Festival of Frost Floats."

Jack nodded knowingly. "It was the only time of the year she really came alive."

"It rang a bell, but I couldn't remember why," Trudy offered. "Not until I saw this photograph." She blinked back tears. "Growing up, my mother struggled to take care of me. Somehow, she held onto me until I hit sixteen, at which point she gave up completely and dropped me off with Aunt Olivia. Gosh, I was resentful. I hated everyone and everything. Aunt Olivia gave me a journal, and I sat in my bedroom and wrote angry poetry and music lyrics, trying to get all the darkness out of my system.

"But one night, around Christmas, Aunt Olivia knocked on my door and asked me to come outside with her," Trudy went on. "I don't know why I left my room. Maybe it was something in Olivia's voice. Maybe I was hungry." Trudy laughed gently. "She tossed my winter coat to me and led me outside. It was a winter wonderland in every sense. Snow floated from the heavens. Christmas floats were decorated with bright lights, trees, Santa Clauses, and carollers, and people threw candy through the darkness so that children could scamper from the sidewalk and collect it. I was probably the angriest teenager in the world, but that night took me out of myself."

Jack's eyes glistened. "You're just remembering this now?"

"I blocked out so much of my teenage years," Trudy explained. "I guess I was trying to protect myself, you know."

Jack nodded.

"Anyway," Trudy continued, her voice breaking. She passed the photograph across the couch and pointed to the woman beside Aunt Olivia. "That woman was there that night. She was all dressed up in a gorgeous fur coat, smiling beautifully. I seem to remember her floating down from one of the Christmas floats and taking me in her arms. It had been ages since I had allowed anyone to hug me. It caught me completely off-guard."

"I can imagine," Jack breathed.

Trudy mopped the tears from her cheek with her sleeve, willing herself to calm down. Every time she closed her eyes, the magical Festival of Frost Floats appeared, its sounds and colors restorative, drawing together the people of Wilmington and Burks Falls.

"I must be going crazy," Trudy continued. "Because I'm thinking about throwing together the Festival myself. I mean, that's insane, right? I haven't even put up the Christmas decorations around the inn! I'm hardly staying afloat."

Jack's smile was crooked and knowing. "You seem like the kind of woman who can do whatever she puts her mind to."

"I don't know about that."

But as Trudy sat in the warm glow of Jack's gaze, she felt as though she floated a few inches above the couch cushions. She couldn't let the Festival of Frost Floats die out this year. She had to make it happen if only to honor Aunt Olivia's memory— and ensure the children in Wilmington and Burks Falls all had Christmas presents under the tree. It was the only way.

# Chapter Five

Burks Falls, New York

Helen Mitchell hated the snow. Bundled up from top to bottom, her winter boots laced tightly, she forced herself into the tundra outside her bungalow, all the way to the mailbox. Sunlight burst from the crisp top of the snowfall they'd gotten last night, making it difficult to see anything. All the way down the block, children scampered through their yards, throwing snowballs and shrieking at the eggshell blue sky. Their joy was foreign to Helen.

Three envelopes awaited Helen in the mailbox: the gas bill, the light bill, and a letter reminding her to sign up for the summertime outdoor symphony subscription. She'd stupidly written her address somewhere and frequently received trash like this.

When Helen returned to her front porch, she stomped the snow from her boots. Just before she bent to unlace them, she heard her name from the house next door.

"Helen!"

Helen groaned quietly and turned to find her neighbor, Beth, waving wildly. She, too, was all dressed up, presumably for her trek to the mailbox. Often, Helen tried to time her mail retrieval for after Beth's, but she hadn't bothered to pay attention today. She cursed herself.

"How about this snow, huh?" Beth cried. Already, she was off her front porch, bursting through the white to reach Helen's porch, her cheeks bright red. "They said we would get seven inches, but I think this is closer to a foot. Don't you?"

Helen didn't care. She didn't care how many inches of white precipitation was on her front lawn. She just wanted to return to the warmth of her living room, drop into a documentary or a TV show, and kill time until dinner.

"Do you have any tea?" Beth asked, adjusting herself on the front stoop of the porch and smiling. "I just baked a bunch of cookies. I'd love to share them."

Helen should have said no. Unfortunately, many years ago, her mother had implanted a level of politeness within her that required her to smile and say, "That sounds nice." Privately, she began to cultivate a plan to get Beth out of her house as quickly as she could.

Helen put the kettle on in the kitchen, listening for the footfalls from the porch that indicated Beth had returned with cookies. This spontaneous visit from Beth wasn't a surprise, necessarily. Ever since Beth's husband had died last year, Beth had made up her mind to befriend Helen, the widow next door. Beth had probably assumed that Helen would assist Beth through the grieving process, explaining what had helped her get through that terribly dark time. Beth had been wrong to think that. Helen had no advice for anyone. She was very sure that regardless of the situation, you were supposed to help yourself and only yourself.

Beth stomped her boots of snow on the front porch and hollered as she entered. "I hope you like oatmeal peanut butter!"

Helen padded into the living room, wearing a pair of slippers, blue jeans, and a thick sweater she'd knitted herself. Beth wore sweatpants, a sweatshirt, and no makeup. When her husband had been alive, Beth had been something of a trophy wife, always wearing bright red lipstick and curling her hair. The difference was striking.

"Oh. They look nice," Helen said as Beth unfurled the top from her Tupperware container. The cookies were strangely formed, as though a child had made them.

"Do you like to bake?" Beth asked.

"Not really," Helen said, although she adored it. She retrieved one of her mother's old china plates from the cabinet, upon which Beth placed her cookies. She was reminded of doing this for her daughter a million years ago after she'd returned home from school. Her cookies had been perfectly round, of course— and her daughter had been so beautiful, with her blonde curls and her little blue dresses with the lace at the edges. Helen had sewed them herself.

Beth and Helen sat in the living room in front of the television, which played a talk show on low volume. Helen wished she could crawl into the screen and join them, becoming somebody else.

"I just love watching the children play in the snow," Beth was saying. "It reminds me of my own children.

Gosh, Billy hasn't been back to Burks Falls all year. And Maggie was here over the summer with her children, but it made her too gosh-darn sad to be at home without her dad around." Beth worried her lower lip and stared into her tea.

This wasn't territory Helen wanted to get into. As an older woman, it stood to reason that so many of her peers had died or were dying. But did everyone have to talk about it all the time? Couldn't it just be an accepted part of life?

Beth was talking about how difficult the holiday season was without her husband around. "I haven't even brought out the Christmas decorations," she said, shaking her head. "I used to always decorate the weekend of Thanksgiving."

Helen rolled her shoulders back and gestured around the living room. "Do you see even a strand of garland, Beth?" She felt rather proud when she said it, as though Christmas was something she'd outgrown.

Beth shook her head sadly. "I realized that when I said it. You haven't decorated your porch for Christmas in years."

"It's just a lot of work for nothing," Helen assured her. "If you don't feel up to it, don't bother yourself. January will be here before you know it."

Beth went on to add that she was going to join her daughter's family for Christmas that year, anyway, and that she wouldn't be around to enjoy her own decorations. "Oh, but it's just broken my heart thinking about the Festival of Frost Floats this year."

Helen sipped her tea. "What about it?"

Beth's eyes glinted, probably because she'd realized

she had gossip Helen didn't. That was the currency in small towns like Burks Falls.

"You didn't hear? Olivia passed away," Beth said. "There's nobody to run the festival this year."

Helen's throat tightened with a surprise rush of nostalgia. When she blinked, Olivia's face floated in her mind's eye: Olivia at twenty-something, her smile enormous, and her laughter echoing through parties, always uniquely her own.

"It was a sudden illness," Beth added. "That's all I know."

Helen sniffed and took a small bite of cookie, surprised at how creamy and buttery it was. She'd expected it to taste of sand.

"They already held the funeral," Beth said. "I thought about asking you to go, but." She paused, searching for words. "I know you and Olivia had that falling out years ago."

Helen finished her cookie and reached for another, surprising herself with how hungry she suddenly felt. Ordinarily, she was focused on nutrition and health. An extra ounce of fat on her body would make her very uncomfortable, she knew.

"I don't know what you want me to say," Helen said suddenly, bristling. "I have nothing good to say about Olivia. It's a tragedy she died so young, of course. The late sixties is no time for that. But death comes for all of us, I suppose. And it was her time."

Beth's eyes were rimmed red with tears. Slowly, she put her mug of tea on the table beside the couch and set her palms over her thighs. Helen had the sensation that she'd just won something but that she'd cheated.

"Do you ever think about forgiving the people who've wronged you over the years?" Beth asked quietly.

Helen raised her shoulders. "I hardly think about anyone at all."

Beth nodded with a sigh. The silence between them was deafening, and Helen itched to reach for the remote and turn up the volume on the television. Beth could stay if she wanted to. She just had to stop talking.

Eventually, Beth got the hint, collected her Tupperware, and returned home. Helen heard herself thank her for the cookies and the conversation, to which Beth gave her a look that meant, *I know you hate me. I'm beginning to hate you, too.* Helen decided not to care.

Later that afternoon, Helen felt the cookies sloshing around her stomach, and she decided to go for a brief walk. The roads had been cleared and salted, and plenty of people were out and about, roaming her street, waddling in winter boots, their bright hats making them look foolish and youthful. Helen donned her practical black coat, black hat, black gloves, and black boots and stepped into the crisp air, where she turned to lock her front door. Nobody else in Burks Falls bothered to lock up. They were idiots. Bad things happened to people all over the world, even in small towns.

For a little while, Helen allowed herself to get lost in her head, marching along the streets of the town in which she'd been born and raised. To her, it was the only place in the world she'd ever wanted to be – and the idea that Beth's children had wanted to move elsewhere was beyond her. She walked past the Presbyterian Church where she and her husband, Brian, had been married decades ago, remembering the soft pearl buttons up the back of her wedding dress, remembering her mother's hand over hers as they'd prayed a final time before she'd gone down the aisle. Both of Helen's parents had died a few years before Brian had died, a quick succession of losses that had taught Helen just how impermanent love and life were. It was best to care for yourself, first and foremost.

When Helen turned the corner between the church and the movie theater, she froze with panic, like a rabbit who'd been discovered in the woods by a hiker. There, on the other side of the street, was Emily. She carried two shopping bags, and she wore a light pink hat that suited her gorgeous blonde hair, which cascaded down her shoulders. It had been several months since Helen had spotted Emily in public, and she was surprised at how much it tugged at her heartstrings.

To Helen's horror, Emily glanced across the street and spotted her, too. She stopped short, adjusting her body toward her and opening her blue eyes wider. She did not smile, perhaps because she didn't want to frighten Helen. But Helen had already turned on her heel, charting a course around the church and back where she'd come from. There was nothing to salvage in that relationship, nothing else to say. It was best not to give anything or anyone too much space in your heart. She knew that.

# Chapter Six

Trudy kept the photograph she'd discovered on her Aunt Olivia's old desk. The three bright-eyed women, the mysterious man, and the beautiful baby, all carrying secrets of a long-ago day of goodwill and joy, were a comfort, if only because they reminded Trudy of all the happiness Olivia had once had in her life. But beyond that, it irritated Trudy to remember that once upon a time, Olivia had been surrounded by so much love— only to die without a real friend to mourn her. What had happened? Why had Olivia's life fallen apart at the seams?

With Jack's help, plus several inn staff member recruitments, Christmas decorations soon adorned every square inch of the place. Wreaths hung on every door; sculptures of angels played trumpets or opened their mouths to carol on high; nativity scenes were set in the foyer, in the dining room, and in the library, and heaps of fake snow were thrown over mantels. Christmas music floated from the speakers, and staff members hummed along as they scurried around the inn, cleaning rooms, vacuuming rugs, or carrying luggage for guests.

"I told you!" A guest said to a friend as they breezed through the foyer. "This place is the ultimate Christmas destination. I feel like it's even more Christmassy than last year, if that's even possible."

Three days after the discovery of the photograph, Trudy again called Monica in Boston to check on the coffee franchise.

"Good as always," Monica assured her. "Nothing to report. How's the inn?"

"I finally feel like I'm getting the hang of things," Trudy said, surprising herself.

"It hasn't even been a week yet! You're a master. Is there anything you can't figure out in no time flat?"

"I just promised myself I would plan and host an entire Christmas Festival," Trudy said. "Which is bound to be a disaster."

"You know it's December 7th, right?" Monica's tone suggested Trudy had lost her mind. Maybe she had.

"I only have about two and a half weeks," Trudy said, wincing.

"What kind of festival?"

"It's a parade. Local businesses pay to feature their decorated floats, and all the proceeds go to charity," Trudy explained. "I have this weird memory of attending one years ago. It really was magical."

"Your aunt handled this, too?"

"She was superwoman. I can't help but think of all she did for me when I had no one else." Trudy said this hesitantly, remembering that she'd never told Monica about her past. But Monica, so far away in Boston, didn't seem to notice.

"I'm sure she'd understand if you can't keep this one tradition going," Monica assured her. "Nobody else stepped up to take over. It doesn't have to be you."

Trudy remained quiet. How could she explain to Monica, an outsider, that she'd already set her heart on putting together the parade? How could she explain that she'd already been bitten by the Wilmington Christmas bug?

But after Trudy got off the phone, she struck gold. In a pile of papers in the corner of her aunt's desk, she found a list entitled **2022 Festival Sponsors**, which included twenty-five businesses that had participated in the festival last year. There was Lickity Split Ice Creamery, Hair Crusaders Barbershop, Pizza Pete, Tacos on Fifth, and The Flannery Pub, amongst so many others, all of whom she could visit over the course of the next few days to ask for continued support. This got her heart going. She glanced at the photograph again, eyeing Olivia knowingly. "Did you put this here for me to find?" she asked quietly, feeling a mix of foolishness and joy.

Before Trudy knew what she was doing, she was behind the wheel of her car, listening to her phone whip directions at her. "Turn left in four hundred feet," the computer's voice instructed. "Make a slight right." It hadn't snowed since the night of her aunt's funeral, but the near foot they'd gotten remained sweeping across front yards, over rooftops, and along the riverbank. She allowed herself to drop deeper into the Christmas magic of the ornate place, hoping it would give her the strength she needed to throw this parade.

Jack's Christmas tree farm was a fifteen-minute drive from the inn. When her phone told her to turn, she initially didn't see the road at all and had to squint to make out tire tracks on a dirt road. Just after she turned, she spotted a big wooden sign, upon which he'd painted: **Jack's Christmas Tree Farm**. Warmth flooded her chest.

It was a Thursday during the middle of the afternoon, which meant the parking lot of the Christmas tree farm was mostly empty, save for that big truck Jack had driven to the inn on the first day they'd met and three other cars. Trudy parked and headed toward the little shack on the other end of the lot, inhaling air heavy with pine, mud, and snow. Long before she reached the shack, Jack burst out from behind the door and waved a big, gloved hand. It had been a long time since anyone had looked so pleased to see Trudy.

"This is a surprise!"

Trudy laughed, filling the air in front of her face with steam. "I had to see this place. You're always going on about it."

"Do I really talk that much?" Jack teased.

Trudy nodded, feigning solemnity. "You really do." She punched him lightly on the bicep just as three guys in their late-teens or early twenties breezed around the side of the shack, one of them with an ax. They peered at them curiously.

"Hey guys," Jack said. "This is Trudy."

"Hey," they mumbled, smiling before they disappeared into the shack.

"They're bored," Jack offered. "But we'll have an uptick after school and work gets out. Mark my words. They'll be cutting Christmas trees right and left."

Trudy laughed. "It seems like a nice job?"

"We have fun," Jack affirmed. "The oldest one, Murphy, has worked with me since he was sixteen. He's twenty-five now. I don't know what I did to deserve his loyalty."

"I have a hunch," Trudy said, giving Jack a soft smile.

Jack shifted his weight from foot to foot, nervous after the compliment. "To what do I owe the pleasure of your visit?" he asked.

Trudy unfurled the note she'd found on her aunt's desk, explaining her plan. "I thought about just calling them, but I think going into each business, explaining that my aunt died and that we only have two and a half weeks to throw this together, seems easier and more personable. I want them to know how much I care. You know?"

Jack nodded and read over the list. "I know a lot of these owners personally."

Trudy's heart lifted. "You think they'll be willing to make a last-minute Christmas float?"

"Absolutely," Jack said. "These people go out of their way for the community." He stuck his tongue into the inside of his cheek, overwhelmed with thought. "It's a nice variety of Burks Falls and Wilmington folks. Some of these businesses have been running for generations."

"I didn't realize the parade went through both Burks Falls and Wilmington?"

"They're so close. Sister cities, you know." Jack winked as he passed the list back to her and glanced toward the shack. The boys inside were cackling at something, a joke they would never share. "Why don't I come with you?"

"What? You don't have to do that." Trudy folded the list nervously. "You're needed here at the farm, aren't you?"

"Murphy's here," Jack explained. "He takes over my responsibilities when I have other stuff to do. When I need to deliver twenty-five Christmas trees to the Hollow's Grove Inn, for example." He laughed.

"But it's probably not something you want to do," Trudy tried to give him another out. "It's going to be a lot of driving around, chatting with people."

"If you haven't noticed, I love driving around and chatting with people," Jack said, his eyes sparkling. "If you don't mind the company?"

Trudy realized, deep in her gut, that the only reason she'd driven out here to show Jack the list was because she'd secretly fantasized about this very set-up. She'd imagined them driving around the snow-capped villages, swapping stories, and listening to the radio. But she hadn't actually thought it would happen.

Jack insisted on driving, as he knew the roads like the back of his hand. Trudy sat in the passenger seat of his truck, shivering, but not because of the cold. Jack turned on the heat as high as it would go and flicked through the radio stations until it played oldies. The soft crackle of the recording loosened Trudy's tight shoulders. She forced herself to breathe.

"Where to first?" Jack asked, waving a final time toward Murphy, who stepped out of the shack to greet an incoming car.

They opted to hit up PTR Credit Union first, an adorable little bank that never would have made it in the big city. Jack parked his truck out front, and Trudy led him inside, where it smelled like chestnuts and cinnamon and was decorated with a little Christmas tree in the corner. The bank tellers wore Christmas sweaters, and their glasses hung from silver strands wrapped around their necks.

"Jack! Good afternoon!" The seventy-something

teller, Gwen, smiled happily as Jack approached. "This is a surprise. Ever since you made an online account, I haven't seen you."

Jack laughed. "Technology has kept us apart, Gwen. I'm sorry about that."

Gwen glanced curiously at Trudy. "And how have you been holding up, Jack?" She asked it with an edge of darkness, as though there was a real reason for the question. As though something horrible had happened.

"Not bad at all. And right now, I have a Christmas project, if you can believe it. You know how I like to stay busy."

Jack introduced Trudy, explaining she was Olivia's niece, here to handle the affairs at the inn and tackle the Festival of Frost Floats. Gwen's eyes got bigger and bigger as he spoke, and by the end of his three-minute tirade, she was nodding excitedly.

"I was so nervous the festival wasn't happening this year! I'd already promised my grandson we could put together a float!"

It was easier than Trudy ever could have imagined. Gwen promised she'd speak with the owner of the bank that afternoon and call them back immediately, but she winked as she said it, as though it was a clear given. "The boss just loves to be involved in the community. We're not some big, faceless bank, you know?"

The rest of their stops that afternoon went similarly. Frequently, the person behind the counter gushed about how much they'd missed Jack, how they hadn't seen him around as much as normal. And nearly every time, they suggested there was something amiss about Jack, as though something had recently gone wrong. One man asked, "And how are things since...?" trailing off as though whatever had happened was too horrific to say. Each time, Jack took the questions in stride, suggesting nothing had ever gone wrong at all.

Trudy remembered Jack telling her he'd been distracted the previous few years. She could only assume these questions had something to do with whatever that distraction was. She burned to ask him— but she didn't want to ruin the mood.

Trudy also couldn't help but notice how many shop owners gave Trudy looks of hope, as though she was the answer to Jack's broken heart. Maybe that was all in her head, though. Maybe she just had a little crush on him, one that bolstered her holiday cheer.

She deserved a little crush, she supposed. She'd spent too many years feeling nothing at all.

# Chapter Seven

After three afternoons of visiting businesses, community centers, and local schools, Jack and Trudy finally reached the end of the list. Not a single business owner or organizer had said no. It was truly sensational.

"After so many years in Boston, I got used to people's nihilism," Trudy admitted, gazing out the window as they drove through downtown Burks Falls. "I guarantee that two-thirds of twenty-five businesses in Boston would have asked me to leave immediately."

"That's so disheartening," Jack said quietly. "How do you stand it?"

Trudy allowed the question to linger in the air for a moment. It wasn't one she could answer, not even privately.

"Gosh, I'm starving." Jack stopped at a red light as soft snow fluttered upon the truck and melted on the front window. To their left was the Burks Falls courthouse, which looked nearly identical to the one in Wilmington, suggesting the two towns were two halves of the same whole. A sleigh with Santa Claus and his reindeer hung over the street, making it look as though he was flying over the town, his arm flung back to wave as he departed.

Before Trudy could chicken out, she heard herself say, "I'm hungry, too. Why don't we go somewhere? Wait." Trudy peered through the snow at an ornate restaurant sign down the road, which advertised Italian food. A couple entered, hand-in-hand, the woman's dark hair dotted with snow. "Do you like pasta?"

"Doesn't everyone?"

Trudy laughed. "There's parking on the street. Pull over!"

Trudy and Jack walked side-by-side in the fading gray light of the winter evening. It was December 10th, just thirteen days before the Festival of Frost Floats, and Trudy imagined the participants across both Wilmington and Burks Falls brainstorming their float decorations and getting creative over hot cocoa. Just before they reached the front door of the Italian restaurant, she said, "Wait! I just realized the inn should have a float. Don't you think?"

"And the Christmas tree farm," Jack affirmed.

"We have work to do!"

"More work?" Jack feigned annoyance. "With you, there's always more to do, isn't there?"

"I'm a workaholic back in the city," Trudy admitted. "When I opened my first coffee shop a million years ago, I was sure that would be enough work. But once it started running smoothly, I opened a second one, then a third. I couldn't stop. Now, it's a franchise across Massachusetts."

Even as she told her personal history, she winced, hoping she didn't come off as arrogant. Instead, as Jack opened the door and gazed into her eyes, he looked at her as though she was the only woman in the world.

"I'd love to go to your coffee shops. I'm sure they're something special."

"I love them. But it's strange. I've hardly thought of them at all since Wilmington took over my life," Trudy admitted, stepping into the warmth of the restaurant, which smelled of warm baked bread, oregano, and melted cheese.

A hostess approached them to ask if they had a reservation. When they said no, she peered down at her table chart as though she was fitting together an intricate puzzle. "Follow me."

Jack and Trudy were led into the back room of the restaurant, where nearly every table was full: husbands and wives sharing bottles of wine, families with toddlers whose cheeks were covered with pasta sauce, and teenage couples holding hands over the table. Their table was located along the wall, where a candle flickered and cast strange shadows across the wall.

"Have you been here before?" Trudy asked Jack as she sat across from him.

"Once or twice," Jack said distractedly, glancing around as he raised the menu.

Trudy suspected that Jack had taken a few dates here over the years. He was a very handsome and charming man. She hoped she wasn't putting him through some sort of emotional wringer, dragging him into this place.

"What's good here?" she asked, hoping to distract him.

"I love the ravioli," he admitted, returning his gaze to hers. "And the chicken parmesan is out of this world."

Trudy laughed, feeling connected to him again. Who cared if he'd brought a date to this restaurant before? This wasn't a date. They were just friends who planned to share a meal together. By the end of the year, she'd be back in Boston, and all of this would be a memory. She might as well enjoy herself.

Trudy ordered ravioli filled with mushrooms and ricotta cheese, while Jack opted for the spaghetti bolognese. Jack suggested they share a bottle of red, which Trudy agreed to. Each time she allowed her eyes to drift away from Jack, she realized that many people were looking at them curiously. Probably, they knew Jack. Probably, they thought Jack was on a date with this stranger. The idea became a warm optimism flowing through her, even though it wasn't true.

After the waiter filled their wine glasses, Jack raised his for a toast. "To our new friendship."

"And to the Festival of Frost Floats," Trudy finished.

"It'll be the best one yet," Jack said, clinking her glass with his.

The wine was delicious, something from a region of Italy Trudy didn't know anything about. When she asked Jack if he knew, he snorted and said, "I've hardly ever left New York State."

"Is that so?" Trudy tilted her head.

"I'm an outdoorsy guy," Jack said. "When I went into the city to drop off that furniture I made, I felt terribly claustrophobic. After the sale, I drove out of there as quickly as I could and had to stop to hyperventilate at the side of the road."

"That's terrible! Oh, Jack. I'm so sorry." Trudy

pressed on her chest, remembering her own hyperventilating episodes and just how much she'd hated her lack of control. She'd thought she was dying.

"It's fine." Jack waved his hand. "My body is very clear about its needs. I guess that's a blessing?"

Trudy sipped her wine and considered this, thinking of how disconnected she'd been from her own body and its needs during the five years since her husband's death. She burned to ask Jack about his past, about what had filled the first nearly fifty years of his life, but she didn't want to darken the mood. Their flirtation was like a cloud, floating them through a fictional world. Jack spoke about light things: his childhood in the same home in which he now lived, his years of playing football, basketball, and baseball, and his appreciation for literature, which surprised Trudy a bit.

"I know," Jack said. "Nobody ever thinks I read."

"It's not that," Trudy stuttered, although it was.

"I spend a lot of time alone," Jack admitted, his eyes shadowed. "I hate the way television makes my brain feel like it's melting, but I love novels."

"Do you have a favorite?"

"I have to pick just one?" Jack asked, feigning shock.

"Okay. You can pick two."

Jack thought for a moment, his lips puckered. "Okay. *The Sea Wolf* by Jack London. And *A Moveable Feast* by Ernest Hemingway."

Trudy leaned back in her chair and crossed her arms. Both books were close to her heart. More than that, her husband had adored both of them.

"I really love Elizabeth Strout, too," Jack admitted. "*Olive Kitteridge* knocked me over."

"You read *Olive Kitteridge?*" Trudy's heart thudded, the sound filling her ears.

"I read just about anything I can find," Jack said.

The idea of this muscular man cozying up with such an open-hearted yet nuanced story nearly shattered Trudy. She didn't know what to say, so she took a long drink of wine and reminded herself she hadn't come to Wilmington to fall in love. Another voice said: *you're not in Wilmington right now, honey. You're in Burks Falls.*

Something bright caught Trudy's eye, and she glanced to her right to find a blonde woman in chef whites weaving through the tables, speaking in low tones. It was Emily, the forty-something woman who'd come to Olivia's wake. When Emily turned to nod to another guest, Trudy raised her hand to catch Emily's attention, fluttering her fingers. When Emily spotted her, her cheeks became blotchy with color. It was unclear if she was happy to see Trudy or not.

But as Emily approached the table, Trudy shuddered with confusion. Although, yes, she'd recognized Emily from meeting her in person, she recognized her from somewhere else, too.

"Good evening." Emily seemed unable to smile. "Trudy, Jack. Welcome. I hope you're enjoying yourselves?"

"I didn't realize this was your restaurant," Trudy said, her voice wavering.

"For the past fifteen years," Emily offered. "Ever since I got back from culinary school."

"It's extraordinary," Trudy said. "Jack told me everything is good here."

"Jack would know. You've probably tried the whole menu at this point, haven't you?"

Jack's cheeks were cherry red. "I love Italian food."

Trudy's stomach tightened with nerves. She reached around the side of her chair to dig through her purse, where she kept the old photograph from the attic pressed in a book. She brought the photograph through the air with a flourish, presenting it to Emily.

"I just realized," Trudy began, "that you look remarkably like two of the women in this photograph."

Emily studied the photo for a long time, her jaw so tight that it looked as though she was hurting herself.

"I found it in the attic of the Hollow's Grove," Trudy went on. "I know the woman on the left is my Aunt Olivia. But I wasn't sure about anyone else. Not until I saw you across the restaurant."

Emily's nostrils flared as she passed back the photograph. Regretfully, she admitted, "You have a good eye."

"You are related to them?"

"I'm the baby in the photo," Emily told her. "The woman holding me is my mother, and the woman beside her is my Aunt Danika. The man is my father."

Trudy felt a rush of excitement. She hadn't imagined she'd be able to solve this puzzle so quickly.

"Have you seen the photograph before?" Trudy asked.

"Never."

Trudy stuttered. "You should have a copy! I can make one and email it to you."

"That's not necessary," Emily said, her eyes hardening.

Across the table, Jack drank his wine a little too quickly as though he was grappling with his own anxiety. Was it possible he'd once dated Emily? But Emily was wearing a wedding ring. Had Emily left him for someone else?

"I remember your Aunt Danika," Trudy interjected, hoping to keep Emily at the table as long as she could. "I have this memory of her and my aunt at the Festival of Frost Floats so many years ago. She was so majestic, wearing a fur coat and floating down the snow-filled streets."

Emily swallowed. "My Aunt Danika was very special. I can hardly talk about her without breaking down."

"I'm so sorry." Trudy treaded lightly. "She passed away?"

"About ten years ago," Emily said. "In her twenties, Aunt Danika founded the Festival of Frost Floats, and it completely transformed the community at Christmas time. People used to call her the Christmas Fairy." A smile played across Emily's lips. "I loved calling her that, too. Anyway, after she died, her best friend took over the festival. Your Aunt Olivia."

Trudy's heart opened. She had the sudden instinct to stand up and hug Emily. They'd been drawn together by these two best friends, who'd now passed on. It was as though she could feel the love Danika and Olivia had had for one another so many decades later.

"Trudy's keeping the festival going," Jack said softly. "We've been hard at work all week, chatting with businesses about their floats."

Emily blinked quickly as though she was on the brink of tears. "My aunt would be so happy. Thank you." Before she could fully fall apart, she tilted her head toward the kitchen, saying, "I better get back there. I can see how hungry Jack is." She cleared her throat. "See you both later."

Emily hurried behind the whipping kitchen door, disappearing into the steam-filled kitchen. Trudy took her wine and swirled it thoughtfully as Jack stared into the middle-distance, lost in thoughts of his own. It was bizarre, Trudy thought now, that she'd been thrust into a world of secrets and memories. Even though Wilmington and Burks Falls were brimming with happy and very kind people, everyone seemed to be protecting themselves from getting hurt. It was mystifying.

# Chapter Eight

Helen was very strict about scheduling her hair appointments. Every six weeks, she went to Peggy's downtown Curly Cues hair salon for a trim and color touch-up, where she sat in a cushioned chair for nearly two hours, drank a glass of chardonnay, and listened to the latest in Burks Falls gossip. It was a ritual, something she clung to, like getting her nails done or doing Pilates in the living room. Back when Brian had been alive, he'd adored her hair, often curling it around his fingers as they'd kissed. She would have hated for him to see her without dyed hair, a little old lady.

Then again, had he lived, he would have eventually gotten old, too. What would he have looked like? It was impossible to know. She hadn't been given that gift.

Peggy greeted Helen with her traditional glass of chardonnay and a smile that showed the gap in her teeth. At forty-something, Peggy had two teenage boys, a husband who worked as a mechanic, and a little house off of Main Street, where she cared for her aging mother. It was not lost on Helen that Peggy was the daughter Helen wished she had.

Then again, Emily had done very well for herself. The Italian restaurant she owned, operated, and cooked for was immaculate and had been written up in countless travel magazines. They'd called Emily a visionary, carving out a new frontier in Italian-American cuisine. Helen hadn't gone to the restaurant, of course, and she never planned to. She had secretly considered ordering food to be delivered, thinking that whoever brought it over wouldn't have known who she was, anyway. But she still hadn't dared.

After Peggy washed her hair, Helen sat with her glass of chardonnay and listened to the other women around her, many of whom she'd known since she was a girl. There was Gina, who'd married the man who operated the bank; there was Quinn, who still ran marathons despite her sixty-some years; and there was Natalie, whose artwork had once appeared in a gallery in New York City. All of them had raised children in Burks Falls, and all of them, incidentally, needed their hair dyed on a consistent rotation. It was terrible, the maintenance involved with getting old— but they handled it well, more or less.

"What did you say they're doing, Gina?" Natalie asked, leaning over the side of her chair, her rosé glinting.

"I think they're doing *How the Grinch Stole Christmas*," Natalie said proudly. "I saw a big Grinch puppet in the garage and nearly screamed my head off."

Natalie chuckled, closing her eyes.

"What's all this about?" Peggy breezed back into the main area, having had to fetch a fine-toothed comb in the back.

"The Festival of Frost Floats," Gina explained.

"Oh!" Peggy stalled behind Helen's chair and smiled into the mirror. "That's right. My boys are doing one for the football team if you can believe it. Although they proved how creative they are over football season..." She trailed off and winked at Helen through the mirror, although Helen had no idea what she was talking about.

"Right! They TP'd so many houses," Quinn said, giggling.

"Even I had to admit that it had some artistry to it. Until I had to clean the yard, that is." Peggy cackled.

"The festival got a late start. But gosh, I'm glad somebody took it upon themselves to make it happen," Natalie said.

Helen's heart sunk into her stomach. For a long time, she scowled at herself in the mirror as Peggy drove the comb through her hair, wiggling the tangles out. When she wielded the sharp scissors, Helen flinched.

"Are you okay, honey?" Peggy asked.

"I'm just fine," Helen assured her, cursing herself for having shown any emotion. She came to the hair salon for personal upkeep and for local gossip. She didn't come to show anyone what she was feeling.

"Just let me know if you need anything," Peggy urged her.

Helen wondered if it was time to find a new stylist.

But more than that, all this talk about the Festival of Frost Floats had drawn her deeper into her memories than she normally allowed herself. Back in the eighties, her older sister, Danika, had had an idea. Helen could practically still see her bursting into Helen's home with that wild smile, announcing, "I'm going to put on a parade."

Helen had called her crazy. "Why would you do something like that?"

Danika sat at the kitchen table next to Emily, who was so small she was trapped in a highchair, babbling. Danika took her hand and kissed it, and Emily squealed happily.

"Do you know how many children in Burks Falls don't get Christmas presents?" Danika asked Helen.

The question surprised her. Helen dropped back against the kitchen counter and folded a towel, eyes to the kitchen tiles.

"I never knew until I started volunteering at the community center," Danika said.

"That's terrible," Helen breathed. "But what does this have to do with a parade?"

Danika outlined her plan: to ask businesses and community organizations across Burks Falls to contribute money and decorate a Christmas float for the festival.

"I'll go as far as Wilmington, too," Danika went on. "The plan is to make it an enormous festival, celebrating all things Christmas. All the proceeds will go toward a toy drive."

Emily squelched and blasted her palms against the plastic table of the highchair. Helen collected Emily in her arms and bobbed her gently, thinking hard about Danika's plan. She'd always known Danika to have far-flung ideas, ones that normal people didn't often come up with. Danika wasn't afraid of hard work, and she'd always had a wild streak— one that hadn't allowed her to settle down and have children, as Helen had already done.

A very small part of Helen wanted to urge Danika to concentrate on other ideas. She wanted to ask Danika if she'd gotten around to calling Victor Perry back, a man who'd been very keen to date her. But another part of her recognized the importance of this parade and toy drive. If Danika was the one to make this happen, Helen was willing to do all she could to help.

Danika called the first "official" meeting for the Festival of Frost Floats that Sunday afternoon. The only two in attendance were Helen and Danika's best friend, the vivacious Olivia. Since Helen was six or seven, Olivia and Danika had been attached at the hip, so much so that Helen regarded Olivia as a second big sister. Olivia, too, was in awe of Danika's strength, promising to do everything she could to make this parade happen.

"I walked around Burks Falls talking to businesses today," Olivia said, clasping her fingers together. "A few people gave me some crazy looks, but a few others were excited. They want to contribute to the community. And Jack's Sub Shack is already planning to make a Christmas float that looks like a massive sandwich." Olivia giggled into her hand, dropping her head back so that her curls cascaded down her back.

"Brilliant, Olivia!" Danika smiled.

"Matt wants to help in any way he can," Olivia continued, speaking of her husband. "Maybe we could make a '1st Annual Festival of Frost Floats' float? Something very Christmassy. Something that represents the spirit of the festival."

"Wonderful," Danika said, taking notes.

"What do you think, Helen? Do you think Brian's business would want to participate?" Danika asked.

"I can't imagine what an accountant firm would put on a Christmas float," Helen said doubtfully.

"A very large calculator," Danika joked.

"Or one of those computers," Olivia suggested. "The huge ones they use to go to outer space."

At this, Danika and Olivia caught one another's gaze and burst out laughing, their stomachs heaving. Helen shifted uncomfortably on the couch, wondering if they were making fun of her. It had always been this way: Danika and Olivia living in their own world, which they only allowed Helen a small glimpse of.

Emily began to cry in the next room, and Helen dismissed herself to cradle her baby, listening to Danika and Olivia banter and giggle. Helen's eyes filled with embarrassing tears. This Festival of Frost Floats was a wonderful thing! Why was she letting the Olivia and Danika show bother her? She was in her twenties, for crying out loud.

It was nearly Thanksgiving, which meant Olivia, Helen, and Danika had to act quickly, brewing up excitement for a festival they hoped to hold the final weekend before Christmas. If they kept to this schedule, they could pass all the funds to the community center for the toy drive, and parents could pick up toys to put under the tree on Christmas Eve.

On Thanksgiving Day, Olivia appeared on the doorstep of Helen and Danika's parents' home, her cheeks bright red with excitement.

"I got a call from the high school last night!" Olivia announced. "They want to sponsor three floats— one for the football team, one for the basketball team, and one for the marching band!"

"Wow!" Danika flew across the foyer and hugged Olivia, shrieking.

Helen and Danika's mother came out of the kitchen wearing oven mitts. "What's all this about, Olivia?"

Danika and Olivia were breathless, talking all over one another to explain. Helen remained off to the side, cradling baby Emily as her mother exclaimed, "Isn't that wonderful?"

As always, their mother saw Danika as a mysterious yet remarkable child, the daughter who amazed her at every turn. "This town will keep this tradition going for generations, Dani," their mother said over Thanksgiving dinner a few hours later. "Every time a float drives down Burks Falls Main Street, they'll say your name!"

"It's not about that, Mom," Danika told her firmly. "I just want this town to pay attention to all of its residents. We've been so lucky, you know? But we're not like everyone here."

Helen knew that Olivia's life had not been as lucky as hers and Danika's. Her father had died when she was very young, and her mother had had to work several jobs to make ends meet. Rumor had it Olivia's sister was off the grid somewhere, that she was addicted to drugs and flat broke. Olivia had once told Danika she was terrified because she'd learned her sister had a daughter, and she was pretty sure she couldn't care for her on her own. Olivia's quest was to bring that daughter to live with her. The problem was, of course, that she had no idea where they were.

The way Danika spoke about the Festival of Frost Floats made Helen's heart open. Under the table, she took Brian's hand and squeezed it, wanting to transport just how lucky and happy she felt with him and Emily by her side.

"Okay," Brian interjected. "We're going to do it. We're going to do a float."

"The accounting firm?" Danika's smile widened. "I thought you weren't interested!"

Brian laughed. "How could anyone not be interested after hearing what you have to say about it?"

"It's going to be magical, Brian," Danika assured him. "And Helen's helping me every step of the way."

"I've just talked to a few businesses," Helen said, shaking her head.

"Are you kidding? You were instrumental in nabbing that ice creamery the other day," Danika reminded her. "And Brian, you know how I get. I've been such an anxious wreck, and Helen always calms me down. But that's just the way of Helen. Even before she had a baby, she was like that."

In the hair salon, forty years after that Thanksgiving Day, Peggy, the hairdresser, exclaimed, "Honey! Are you okay?"

Helen bucked up, her eyes widening, and her cheeks streaked with tears. She'd been so lost in her memories, throwing herself through her own personal sorrows, that she'd completely forgotten where she was.

"I'm fine," Helen said, nearly choking on her tears.

Natalie, Quinn, and Gina gaped at her on the other side of the salon. Helen knew they would gossip about this later, probably calling Helen "that lonely, strange old woman." Helen couldn't care about them.

"I had something in my eye," Helen explained. "It must have been the hair chemicals."

# Chapter Nine

Trudy worked the front desk of the Hollow's Grove most mornings and early afternoons, tending to the crackling fire in the fireplace in the sitting room, watching the snow flicker past the bay window, and passing out little maps to guests, instructing them where to shop, where to eat, and where to walk for best views of the surrounding mountain range, capped with snow. The wide range of guests at the inn was fascinating— everyone from married couples in their sixties, seventies, and eighties to young families with toddlers to bright-eyed newlyweds who were hardly able to leave one another's side for more than a few minutes. Trudy remembered those days with her husband, how the idea of spending a few nights away from him had rendered her heartbroken. The concept of becoming a young widow had never occurred to her.

On Wednesday afternoon, Frankie breezed in to take over the front desk and placed a large platter of iced cut-out cookies in front of Trudy. Trudy inspected an iced

Christmas tree, saying, "The icing is nearly an inch thick, Frankie!"

"It's the holidays," Frankie assured her. "Anything without that much icing is criminal."

Trudy took a small bite and closed her eyes at the onslaught of cream, sugar, and dough. "Frankie! You're extraordinary," she told her as Frankie beamed. "Have you ever considered doing this for a living?"

"No! Never. I adore baking around Christmas time, but it's a labor of love for me," Frankie explained. "If it became my job, I would find a way to hate it."

"You don't hate working here," Trudy pointed out.

"Who could hate working here?" Frankie asked with a wave of her hand.

Frankie unbuttoned her winter coat, her eyes glinting with the sunlight of the gorgeous December afternoon. Beneath her coat, she wore yet another Santa sweater as though her closet was nothing but celebratory knits.

"Good afternoon!" Frankie called to the newlyweds, who breezed through the foyer, their fingers intertwined. "Where are you off to today?"

The young woman of the pair had shining red hair and green eyes, and when she spoke, her accent was lilting. Was she actually Irish?

"We're headed out for a small hike," she said, glancing back toward her husband. "Nothing too sporty, though. And Fred has promised me we'll drink plenty of hot cocoa afterward."

Fred beamed at his wife and wrapped his arm around her shoulders. Trudy could see their future flung out before them— the babies they would have, the holidays they would share. There would be hard times, too; there always were. Oh, she hoped they would always maintain the intensity of their love. It was a rare thing to cling to. She knew that.

"I just had the best hot chocolate of my life," Trudy said. "At this little coffee shop just off the river. Betty's Cake Emporium. You have to check it out."

"Intriguing," the Irish woman breathed. "Thank you for the tip."

"Would you like a cookie before you go?" Frankie asked, tilting the platter toward them. The woman selected a candy cane cut-out, and her husband went for a reindeer.

"It's like a Christmas fantasy land around here," the woman said, her eyes aglow.

Just as the newlyweds departed for the afternoon, Trudy's phone buzzed with a message from Jack.

JACK: You said you don't work this evening, correct?

JACK: I'd like to invite you out to the tree farm.

JACK: I have a surprise for you.

Frankie's voice rang out through the foyer. "Look at that smile!"

Trudy raised her chin as nerves rocketed through her chest. It took every bit of force to put her smile away.

"Tell me," Frankie said conspiratorially. "What's made you so happy?"

"It's just this place. Wilmington is so magical," Trudy half-lied, pocketing her phone and drawing her hair into a messy ponytail. She felt as though she could run five miles at once, all the way out to the Christmas tree farm. Jack's text messages had ignited her.

Frankie chuckled and shook her head in disbelief. "Your aunt would have been over the moon to hear you say that." She paused to scrape a few cookie crumbs from the sleeves of her sweater. "The entire town is talking about you, you know. They're terribly pleased with your work for the festival. There's a plan in place to kidnap you if you ever return to Boston."

Trudy laughed delicately, realizing she hadn't thought concretely about returning to Boston in quite some time. She'd thrown herself so completely into the Festival of Frost Floats and her work at the inn. She couldn't even remember the last time she'd called Monica to ask about The Lucky Bean. What had gotten into her?

Trudy drove all the way out to the Christmas tree farm with a smile plastered across her face. She'd forgotten her sunglasses at the inn, and the light reflecting on the heaps of snow flashed into her eyes, nearly blinding her. She didn't care. When she reached the parking lot of the farm, Jack burst from the shack, his grin matching hers. She had the instinct to race into his arms and burrow her face in his chest— but she resisted it, thank goodness.

"Afternoon!" she called as she approached. "What's all the fuss about?"

Jack laughed and tugged his winter hat off his full head of curls. "Check this out. The boys and I have been working on it all week."

Jack led Trudy around a football-field-sized area of trees, most of which weren't ready for Christmas yet. "They'll be perfect by next year," he explained as they rounded the corner.

Behind the trees, Jack and his employees had stationed a parade float, upon which they'd created a gorgeous display. Using papier-mâché, they'd created a massive statue of Paul Bunyan, complete with a red-and-white checkered shirt, a thick black beard, and an ax. Around him on the parade float were Christmas trees from the farm, most of them too scrawny or ill-shaped to be displayed in people's living rooms. Above the statue was a sign that read: **JACK'S CHRISTMAS TREE FARM.**

"Jack! Look at this!" Trudy cried, circling the float slowly, her shoes creaking in the snow. "I had no idea you had so much artistic talent!"

Jack's cheeks were pink, perhaps with embarrassment or perhaps just from the chill. "It's not just me. The boys helped, too."

"But it was your idea," Trudy pointed out.

Jack raised his shoulders. "You got me excited about this festival. I couldn't help but take part."

"You're after that top prize, aren't you?"

Every year at the Festival of Frost Floats, residents of Wilmington and Burks Falls voted on floats, with prizes given out for Most Creative, Silliest, Most Beautiful, and Most Christmassy.

"I'm after that 'Silliest' prize," Jack joked. "And I have an in with the festival organizer. I'd better get what I want."

Trudy laughed. "I have no interest in cheating."

"I guess I'll just have to win the honest way, then," Jack said.

Trudy gazed up at the sculpture of Paul Bunyan, his stoic expression, his firm jaw. "He looks like you," she said.

"That's what the boys said, too."

"Is that why you got into the Christmas tree business?" Trudy asked. "Because you already look like Paul Bunyan?"

"What can I say? I was born into the role," Jack quipped.

Trudy and Jack held one another's gaze for a moment, both of them breathing deeply, filling the air with steam. So far away from the parking lot and shack, Trudy felt as though she and Jack were tucked away in the woods, far from civilization. Overhead, a hawk breezed past, casting shadows across their faces.

"Listen," Jack said, interrupting Trudy's reverie. "Would you like to go downtown with me? I'm about done for the day."

"I'd like that very much."

Trudy and Jack drove separately, with Trudy following behind him in her little car, sensing he drove slower than normal, guiding her safely to a downtown parking lot. From there, they walked along the river, watching several fishermen flash their lines over the water. Jack explained that his father had been a prominent fisherman before his death and that he'd taken Jack out on oceanic fishing trips that had terrified him.

"I'm a mountain man," he explained. "As far as I'm concerned, the ocean doesn't want anything to do with us, and I don't want anything to do with it."

Trudy laughed, surprised that Jack was frightened of anything.

"And you?" Jack asked. "Are you afraid of anything?"

"Almost everything," Trudy said.

"I don't believe that for a second."

At that moment, Trudy wanted to tell him absolutely everything: that she'd been raised in poverty, that she'd fought tooth and nail to get out of her circumstances, that just when she'd allowed herself to relax into her life, Ben had died. It was enough to terrify her into the belief that nothing would ever be good again.

And yet, here she was, on the riverbank with Jack. Didn't that disprove her fears?

Jack eventually led Trudy to a little bar near the riverbank, where a woman with a bright-red dye job served them hot mulled wine with orange slices floating inside. Despite the cold, they sat on the patio with their hands wrapped around their hot mugs, watching the river sweep past.

"I can't wait to show you the mountains in the spring," Jack said, speaking of a future Trudy wasn't sure she believed in. "The falls are extraordinary. Do you have a good pair of hiking boots?"

Trudy laughed. "I've been a city girl for twenty-eight years."

"Does that mean no?"

"It means my idea of hiking has been walking up and down Fifth Avenue."

Jack closed his eyes as he burst into laughter. "We have to change that."

After they finished their first round of mulled wine, Jack retreated inside to order them another and use the bathroom. Trudy remained in the silence of herself, daring herself to imagine a world in which she actually did remain in Wilmington. What did hiking boots look like, anyway? Were they big and bulky? Would they make her look wild?

The bartender came outside with two mulled wines with extra-thick slices of orange. "You two look like you're having a mighty nice time."

Trudy smiled. "It's been fun. The wine is so tasty."

The bartender lingered, her eyes on the snow-capped mountains. "You're sticking around, are you?"

Although Trudy had never met this bartender, it was clear she understood who she was and what circumstances had brought her to Wilmington.

"I'm not sure," Trudy answered. "I have a coffee franchise in Boston."

The bartender's eyes flickered. "You'd better take care of Jack's feelings in all this," she said cryptically. "The boy's been through a lot. He can't take any more heartache, you know?"

Jack returned to the patio, rubbing his palms together. "That was quick! Thanks a lot, Rita."

"Anything for Jack," Rita sang. "You'll holler if you want anything to eat, won't you? I have fresh bread, sliced meat, cheese, olives?"

"This is turning into a classy establishment," Jack teased.

Rita swatted him. "It's always been classy, you son of a gun. I'll make you both some grilled sandwiches, shall I? Nobody drinks on an empty stomach on my watch."

Trudy watched her retreat into the shadows of the old bar as Jack sat back down and spoke about Rita. Apparently, her father had owned the bar before her, and his mother had operated the bar before him. Rita had a real sense of pride about the old place— and often thought of her regulars as part of her family.

"She asked me once or twice to take over the bar for her after she's gone," Jack said sadly. "She never had children of her own."

Trudy shivered with questions about what Rita had alluded to. What heartache had Jack been through? Why did all of Wilmington and Burks Falls fear for his feelings so much? Wasn't he a forty-something man? Couldn't he take care of himself?

Then again, nobody could really take care of themselves alone. Not really. Trudy, the loneliest woman in all of Boston, knew that better than anyone.

The grilled sandwiches were exquisite, the cheese coming out of the bread in melted strings, and the bread buttery and the perfect shade of brown. Trudy heard herself telling Jack more stories from her past, about the mistakes she'd first made when she'd opened the coffee franchise and about a cat she'd owned in her twenties who'd been addicted to cheese. The strange knot in her stomach began to unravel. Once, Jack touched her hand on the table, and her soul floated out of her body.

But on the walk back to the parking lot, everything became much more complicated. There, against a tree that draped its limbs over the bubbling river, Jack turned toward Trudy, touched her elbow, took a large step toward her, and kissed her. The movement happened all at once, a wonderful rush of feeling, and Trudy's knees popped out beneath her, threatening to cast her to the ground. His lips were warm and thick, his breath hot. The kiss couldn't have lasted any longer than five seconds, but it was as though the earth stopped spinning on its axis. Afterward, Jack kept his face close to hers so that all she could see were his eyes, his nose, and his thick black beard.

"I hope that was okay?" He sounded tentative.

"It was more than okay," Trudy whispered.

Jack's smile widened. Tenderly, he wrapped his gloved hand around hers, and they walked silently back to the parking lot, hand-in-hand. Trudy felt just as blissful as the newlyweds at the Hollow's Grove Inn. She felt twenty-five years younger, aglow with optimism and the promise of what came next.

Perhaps reality would crash in on them soon, reminding them of the devastations of their pasts, of how difficult it was to ever outrun yourself. But those feelings would come later. Here and now, Trudy felt the optimism that comes with new love. She'd never imagined it would come for her again.

# Chapter Ten

Helen didn't like to go grocery shopping more than once a week. She always drove there on Tuesday mornings around nine-thirty— when the aisles were clear and well-stocked, and the only other person in the entire store was the twenty-something woman at the check-out counter. As she swiped Helen's yogurt, salmon, avocado, blueberries, and wholegrain cereal, she chewed her gum glumly, her eyes glazed. Although Helen and the young woman saw one another every week at this time, they never said anything more than what was necessary. It was the best relationship Helen had with anyone.

Helen thanked the young woman and wheeled her grocery cart toward the exit, where the doors sprung open just for her. She'd parked in the second row of an empty parking lot, where she journeyed now, her chin raised against the sharp chill. When she returned home, she planned to eat a container of yogurt and read a romance novel. It would kill the rest of the morning.

But just before she reached her car, she stepped on a

patch of black ice. The grocery cart flung out in front of her, and her feet shot out on either side, forcing her to maneuver awkwardly, trying to catch herself. When she did, she flopped to her right and landed on her wrist. There was a terrible crack. Pain rocketed through her arm, up her neck, and into her head. But she wasn't accustomed to making any noise. The idea of screaming, even when she was in such pain, didn't make any sense to her.

Because the grocery store parking lot was empty, Helen eventually forced herself back to her knees. She shook violently, probably because of shock. She tried to rationalize the experience, telling herself this sort of thing happened all the time. Maybe she was officially old. Maybe this was proof.

Helen limped back into the grocery store, where the woman at the check-out counter stared at her phone and chewed her gum. Eventually, Helen cleared her throat and said, "Excuse me? Can you please help me?" And then, she fell against the table against the wall, shivering in a way that clearly frightened the young woman.

The grocery clerk panicked and called 9-1-1, which seemed like overkill to Helen. She still hadn't managed to look at her wrist, not fully, but she had to assume it didn't look quite right. The grocery clerk said plenty of stuff to her, attempting to assure her everything would be all right.

"Of course it will be," Helen said, sounding angry. "Everything is always fine."

When the grocery clerk realized Helen's food remained in her cart, which had wheeled itself to the middle of the parking lot, she hurried outside to retrieve it. By the time she returned, the ambulance had arrived, and she assured Helen she would put everything in the fridge in the back.

"You can pick it up when you're all patched up," the clerk told her with more animation than Helen had ever seen.

The EMT workers checked her vital signs and took her to the hospital. Throughout, she sat upright on the gurney as pain pulsed from her wrist. She'd said something not very kind to one of the EMT workers, and he looked glum, as though he'd expected every little sixty-something-year-old woman to act like Mrs. Claus. But no, Helen thought now. Older women were people, too. They had bad days. They said the wrong things. It just so happened that Helen hadn't said the "right" thing in many years.

It was a slow day at the Burks Falls Hospital. A chipper doctor with a Christmas tie tended to her almost immediately, taking an X-Ray of her wrist, setting the bone, and securing it with a cast. "It should mend in six weeks," he explained. Six weeks was nothing, Helen told herself as she swallowed a pain killer. She would hardly notice the time passing.

But when Helen approached the front desk to hand over her insurance card, Emily popped up from the line of chairs in the waiting area. Her eyes were rimmed red, as though she was panicked, and her hair was frizzy from being under her winter hat.

"Mom!" Emily hurried toward her, her coat whipping out behind her.

"Emily. What are you doing here?" Helen frowned and glanced toward the front desk employee as though she could explain this.

"They called me," Emily rasped.

"Who? Who called you?" None of it made any sense to Helen. She hadn't told anyone to call anyone. She'd always been able to take care of herself.

"The hospital!" Emily looked exasperated. "They said you hurt yourself in the grocery store parking lot." She eyed the cast, her face falling. "Does it hurt? How do you feel?"

"It's just a small break," Helen said. "Nothing major. I'll be fine."

"Let me drive you back to the store to get your car," Emily insisted.

"I'm happy to call a cab," Helen said.

"Mom, there aren't any cabs in Burks Falls."

"I'll take the bus, then."

"You won't take a bus in your condition," Emily said firmly. She tugged her hair and glanced at the hospital employee, who pretended to be busy with something else. Under her breath, she said, "Just let me help you, Mom. I want to."

"And I'm telling you not to bother."

Emily's blue eyes glinted menacingly. "I see you haven't changed."

Helen felt as though she'd been smacked. "Why would I have changed?" She maneuvered around Emily and placed her insurance card on the desk. "I'd like to get this taken care of, please. Unlike my daughter, it's not my preference to hang around in hospital waiting rooms."

Emily waited behind Helen throughout the exchange, jangling her keys. It was clear she wouldn't take no for an answer.

"You can drive me," Helen said as she turned, unable to look her daughter in the eye.

"Wonderful." Emily's voice was hard. "Let's go."

Emily drove a different vehicle now, a big, white SUV that Helen found to be garish.

"Why do you need so much space?" Helen asked as she buckled her seatbelt.

"I visit local farmers for the restaurant. I needed more space to transport ingredients." Emily started the engine and glanced at Helen. "You know, you should really come to the restaurant sometime. I can reserve a table for you."

"I prefer to eat at home."

Throughout the drive to the grocery store parking lot, Emily and Helen hardly spoke. Helen touched her cast gingerly, wondering if the pain would return and keep her from sleeping that night. She often went to bed by eight-thirty, bored in that house alone.

In front of several businesses in Burks Falls, festival floats were stationed, awaiting the approaching parade. They were decorated with various themes: Charlie Brown and Snoopy, Snow White and the Seven Dwarves, and Hansel and Gretel. Although Helen never would have admitted it, some of them looked exquisite, as though professional artists had swooped into Burks Falls to take the reins.

"I can't believe they're still having that stupid Christmas festival," Helen said, flaring her nostrils.

Emily pulled into the grocery store parking lot and shut off the engine next to Helen's car. "You know how much Aunt Danika loved that festival," she said very quietly.

Helen rolled her eyes. There was so much Emily couldn't possibly understand about the past.

"Will you think about coming to the restaurant?" Emily pushed it, her voice startlingly sweet.

Helen swallowed. "Maybe. After the holidays. The

crowds are too much for me right now." With that, she opened the door and stepped into the frigid air. Very carefully, she closed the door behind her and headed back into the grocery store to collect her food. The black ice spot had been fenced off and covered with salt. By the time she returned to the parking lot, Emily's ugly SUV was gone. The nightmare of the day was over. It was time to return home, to hide from a world that, for whatever reason, hadn't fully given up on her yet.

# Chapter Eleven

Jack's kiss both terrified and captivated Trudy—demanding of her a new sense of reality and a fresh way of looking at the world. She hadn't felt capable of it, not in the previous five years of life without her husband. All throughout Thursday, she floated through the Hollow's Grove Inn, greeting guests with a smile too big for her face and taking frequent breaks in the back office to try to get her heart to stop beating so quickly. When Frankie saw her that afternoon, she asked, "Are you sick, honey? You're flushed. You'd better sit down and eat something."

Just like many women falling in love, Trudy had forgotten to eat. Promising Frankie she would take better care of herself, she breezed into the dining room, took a seat at a two-person table with a flickering candle, and perused a menu. Max, the waiter, approached happily to take her order.

"Red wine, butter chicken, and naan bread?" Max scribbled the order onto a pad of paper.

"Thank you, Max." Trudy passed him her menu and

rubbed her temples. "How are you holding up? I hope it isn't too crazy in here?"

"We've found an order in the chaos," Max said with a laugh. "And people are more than understanding around the holidays, thankfully. Especially when we promise them free dessert."

"I'll need some of that dessert, too," Trudy said. "The guests have been raving about it."

Max blushed and leaned closer. "It's my mother's recipe. I passed it along to the chef."

"Your mother is a genius."

"Turns out she and Frankie use similar methods," Max joked. "They lather everything with a little too much icing."

"That works for me."

Trudy sipped her glass of wine and allowed her thoughts to roam, flitting through images of Jack in the winter wonderland of his Christmas tree farm, his thick beard flecked with snow. She thought of his warm lips upon hers, of his strong arms wrapped around her small frame, protecting her. She dared to dream of a night wherein he held her as she slept, as a winter wind barrelled against the house. It was probably too much to hope for, yet here she was, surrounded by Hollow's Grove Inn guests in the cozy restaurant, praying for a future in which she didn't feel half so alone.

"Hello! We'd love a table for four?" A blonde woman in her mid-twenties appeared at the hostess station, carrying a little girl against her chest. A little boy a year or two older than the girl stood beside her leg stoically, clinging to the fabric of her dress, and a handsome man with dirty-blonde hair was behind them, a sturdy shadow.

"Of course," the hostess said, collecting two adult menus and two children's menus. "Right this way."

The family was seated at the table directly next to Trudy's, with the little girl in a highchair and the little boy bravely taking an adult chair for himself. The husband buckled the little girl into her highchair and tied a bib around her neck as the mother pulled several crayons from her purse and set the little boy up with a coloring book. It warmed Trudy's heart to watch a family so in-tune with one another, their every decision an act of care and love.

"You know," the mother said to the little boy as he colored, "I used to live here when I was your age."

The boy blinked up at his mother, his crayon poised. "Here?"

"At the inn," the woman said, smiling. "After dinner, sometimes, my mother would move all these tables to the walls so that we could have a dance party."

The boy looked vaguely impressed. "Can we have a dance party later?"

His mother giggled. "I don't know, buddy. I don't live here anymore."

"Do you remember which room you lived in?" her husband asked.

"I was trying to figure that out when we checked in," the woman said. "I think we mostly spent time on the third floor, but I can't be sure. Mom and I had to move around a little bit, depending on where Aunt Danika wanted us."

An alarm went off in Trudy's mind. Again, she thought of the photograph of Aunt Olivia, Aunt Danika, and baby Emily, taken so long ago. How did this young woman fit into that dynamic?

"Excuse me? I'm sorry to interrupt," Trudy heard herself say.

The blonde woman turned to smile at Trudy. It seemed unlikely that she was ever anything but very kind and pleasant, a model wife, mother, and friend.

"Hi," the woman said, a question in her voice.

"I heard you say you're related to Danika?"

The woman's smile widened. "I am! She was my great-aunt. Did you know her?"

"I met her," Trudy answered, stirring with questions. "A long time ago. My aunt was Olivia, her best friend."

A shadow passed over the young woman's face. She turned to say something to her husband, then rose to walk toward Trudy's table. "I was sorry to hear about Olivia. She was a remarkable woman. The way she took over this inn after Aunt Danika passed was extraordinary. It was a true act of friendship and love.

"Thank you for saying that." Trudy felt a wave of sorrow.

"We booked this vacation here at the Hollow's Grove a few months ago," the woman went on. "When I heard about Olivia's death, I was worried the inn would shut its doors for good. But here it is. Still open. Still magical." She frowned. "I'm assuming you're handling things these days?"

"That's right. I'm Trudy."

"I'm Nina."

"And your mother is Emily?"

Nina nodded. "Have you met her?"

"I went to her restaurant last week. It was divine!" Before Nina could make an excuse and return to her table, Trudy retrieved the photograph from her purse and handed it to her, watching as Nina's face transformed, her eyes heavy with confusion. "I found this photograph in the attic when I first arrived. According to your mother, that's her as a baby. Aunt Olivia is on the left, Danika is beside her, and Emily's mother, your grandmother, is holding Emily. Isn't it an extraordinary photograph?"

A deep wrinkle formed between Nina's eyebrows. "Gosh. I don't think I've ever seen a photograph of Danika and Helen together."

"Really?" Trudy's confusion mounted. She remembered how dark Emily's face had gotten when she'd shown her the photograph last week, as though it represented far more than just a happy day long ago.

"My Grandma Helen and my mother don't speak," Nina said sadly, passing the photograph back as though she wanted to be rid of it, too.

"That's terrible!" Trudy stuttered. "Do you know what happened between them?"

"My mother got pregnant with me when she was still a teenager," Nina said tentatively. "My grandmother was very upset, of course. She has a set idea about the way the world is supposed to go, and she doesn't like to deviate from the plan. But when my mother refused to marry my father, my Grandma Helen became outraged. She told my mother she wouldn't help raise me at all, thinking that would force my mother to marry my father in the end. But ultimately, Aunt Danika swooped in and said my mother could raise me here, at this beautiful inn."

Trudy had never imagined this story before. The history of the old place intensified, and her heart felt strained with sorrow at what Emily's mother had done.

"Of course, Aunt Danika was more of a grandmother than Grandma Helen ever was," Nina went on. "I was devastated when she died so young. Grandma Helen came to her funeral, but she sat way in the back and refused to talk to anyone. Rumor has it that she was quite enraged that Danika left the inn to your Aunt Olivia instead of someone in the family."

"Your grandmother sounds like a very confusing woman," Trudy said.

"My mother doesn't know what to do with her," Nina agreed. "She's tried several times to mend their relationship, but Grandma Helen won't have it. She's content to live her life alone." Nina said as she stared at the carpet. Behind her, her son called for her as he'd finished his first drawing and needed her approval.

"I've taken up too much of your time," Trudy said, reaching out to take Nina's hand. "But thank you for telling me this. It's helped me connect the dots a bit."

"Of course," Nina said. "I'll be here another few days before we join my mother in Burks Falls. I wanted my children to feel the magic of this old inn. Thank you for keeping it alive."

Trudy's butter chicken arrived after that, giving her something else to fixate on besides the chaos of Nina's family's story. Within Nina's face, she could find traits of Danika, Emily, and Helen— women in a tremendously complicated family.

It occurred to Trudy that Olivia had probably thought of them as her own family. Her father had died young; her mother had been difficult, running herself ragged from one job to the next; and her sister had taken off at a young age, resulting in drug addictions and poverty. Olivia had had no one— until Trudy had come to live with her. By then, Olivia's own husband, Matt, had abandoned her. Rumor had it that he'd gone out west.

More and more, Trudy recognized the heart and

strength that had kept Aunt Olivia going. As Danika's story unfolded, she felt closer to a past they'd all abandoned. She wondered if it was possible to bring them back together again in honor of Danika and Olivia's friendship. Couldn't they see how important their love had once been?

It wasn't like Trudy to meddle in other people's businesses. The previous five years, she'd done nothing more than ensure her coffee franchise was running, paid her bills, gone running, fed herself, and cleaned her apartment. She'd felt time creep past as the rest of the world had gone on without her.

As she chewed a bite of naan, she again peered at the photograph of the three beautiful women at the prime of their lives. Only one of them remained alive – and she no longer spoke to the baby in the photograph. The fact of this cratered through Trudy's heart.

Had Helen seen this photograph since it had been taken? Wouldn't it ignite something in her, a memory of a time of warmth and love?

## Chapter Twelve

It was Jack's idea to go to the local zoo. That evening, cheeks flushed with excitement, he appeared at the Hollow's Grove Inn, his heart on his sleeve as he followed Trudy around the sitting room. Bent on doing anything he could to help her, he put away puzzles and games a group of children had left out, added kindling to the fire, and swept up the foyer. It seemed like he'd collected hundreds of stories to tell her, just in the day they'd spent apart. Trudy, too, told him about the guest interactions she'd had, her new trick for making better hot chocolate, and her belief that the attic really was slightly haunted. It felt as though this was the millionth conversation of their lives – one they just extended day after day.

As Jack bent to place the dustpan in front of a pile of dirt, he said, "The Christmas lights at the zoo are absolutely stunning. And they have red pandas! You have to see the red pandas!"

Trudy could have told him she would have gone wherever he wanted to go— the top of a mountain, the coffee shop, a gas station, Timbuktu. She would have followed him anywhere.

"I've never been to the zoo," she told him.

Jack's eyes bugged out of his head. "You're kidding!" He threw out the contents of the dustpan and put the broom away, stuttering with surprise. "That means there are so many animals you've never seen in real life before. Giraffes? Big snakes? Hippos?"

"None of the above," Trudy affirmed, snapping her palms together.

"I don't know what to say!"

Trudy laughed and touched his bicep, which always surprised her with its girth. "I guess I'm in for a surprise, aren't I?"

"The surprise of your life," Jack said.

Jack picked her up the following day at four-thirty, when the afternoon light began to shift toward blues and purples and snow clouds bundled up on the horizon. The drive to the zoo was twenty minutes, during which time Trudy and Jack's conversations were like popcorn, bursting with excitement and spontaneous anecdotes.

Jack and Trudy stood in the soft light of the early evening, analyzing the large wooden map of the zoo near the entrance. Around them, the Christmas light display had begun to pop on, illuminating trees and fences with blues, purples, reds, yellows, and greens, and families ambled around, their children dressed in so many layers that they were forced to waddle. Mothers took too many photographs, forcing children to stand in front of the orangutans and the seals, smiling till their cheeks ached.

"You have to decide what you want to see first," Jack explained. "Making me decide is too much pressure."

Trudy traced her finger along the map, from the

elephant enclosure to the giraffes to the antelopes. "I hope they're all inside?"

"They are," he explained. "At least for the winter. In summer, they have so much ground to cover that it's sometimes hard to figure out where they are."

"You're a zoo expert," Trudy teased.

"I've been here a time or two," Jack admitted. "As a kid, I was obsessed with animals. I begged my mother to bring me all the time, and I always peppered her with facts about them."

"What's your favorite animal fact?" Trudy asked, touching his gloved hand with hers.

Jack smiled and removed both his gloves, then hers, so that they could join hands. Trudy's heart fluttered. For a moment, she thought she might faint.

"Gosh. How can I choose?" Jack rubbed his beard thoughtfully. "There's a very strange lizard that can shoot blood from its eyes."

Trudy wrinkled her nose. "Why on earth would they do that?"

"To confuse their predators."

Trudy couldn't help but smile despite her disgust. "That sounds like a fact a little boy would love."

"You're speaking to a man who used to be a little boy," Jack joked.

"Tell me a nice fact," Trudy begged.

"Okay. Okay." Jack thought for a moment, and Trudy imagined him diving through pages and pages of animal facts, which he kept alphabetized in his mind. "Do you know what a group of parrots is called?"

"No."

"It's called a pandemonium."

"You made that up!" Trudy cried.

"I didn't." Jack's body shook with laughter. "But isn't it nice?"

"It's lovely. A pandemonium."

"Another fact," Jack continued, his eyes sparkling, "is that otters hold hands as they sleep, floating along water side-by-side." He gave her hand a healthy squeeze, and Trudy's eyes filled with tears that she immediately blinked away. It was almost too much.

As they walked toward the first enclosure, an indoor bird exhibition with more than thirty species, Trudy eyed passers-by with wonder, marveling that Jack wanted to be at the zoo with her. To outsiders, they were seen as a couple, hand-in-hand, illuminated with Christmas lights. Perhaps people assumed they were married or engaged, or that they had children in college, or that they'd been dating for years. Perhaps they didn't see a woman overwhelmed with grief who'd buried her husband five years ago.

Over the course of a few hours, Jack and Trudy saw everything: giraffes, their necks long and pulsing as they walked ploddingly through their enclosure, eating little pellets of food from troughs; zebras, sleek and sporty. Jack explained that no two zebras had the exact same stripes, which boggled Trudy's mind. Trudy admitted, after a brief perusal of the snake house, that she wasn't so keen on snakes, on their massive bodies that seemed like long, single muscles. Their orange eyes seemed to pierce through her, sending a shiver down her spine. Jack led her out immediately and bought her a hot apple cider, telling her that he'd been fascinated with snakes as a kid, but he didn't have much time for them these days.

"That's right," Trudy remembered. "You're here for the red pandas! Let's head there next."

When they reached the red panda enclosure, Jack pointed at their little, adorable faces, demanding, "Tell me you wouldn't want one as a pet. Come on! They're cuter than kittens."

Trudy laughed. "They'd climb all over everything!"

"Is that a bad thing?" Jack asked.

As they watched, one of the red pandas burst from a lower limb to the very top, walking the limb as though it were a tightrope.

"I could watch them all day," Jack said, his eyes illuminated with the blue Christmas lights along the nearby tree.

"Maybe you should adopt a few for the Christmas tree farm," Trudy suggested. "Imagine them leaping through the trees! People would come from all over to watch them."

"That would be a dream," Jack said wistfully as Trudy cackled at the image in her mind's eye— of Jack dressed as Paul Bunyan with a red panda on his shoulder.

When the tips of their fingers were numb with cold, Jack led Trudy to the little zoo restaurant, where they ordered burgers, fries, and another round of hot ciders and breathed into their hands to warm up.

"How do you like your first trip to the zoo?" Jack asked. "I still can't believe that. How old are you?"

"Forty-six," Trudy admitted, taking a sip of hot cider.

"Forty-six years without ever seeing a zebra," Jack joked. "Should be illegal."

"I'll truly never forget my first time."

Jack's cheeks were pink. He rubbed his palms together, then tugged at the zipper of his coat. "I can't help but think..." He trailed off. "I don't know. I hope this isn't too forward. I just haven't been able to stop thinking about you since the other day."

Trudy's heart pounded.

"I hadn't kissed anyone in a long time," Jack admitted sheepishly.

"Neither had I."

Jack's eyes widened with surprise. "I figured you have this wild city life in Boston. I mean, you're gorgeous, and you own your own business."

Trudy hesitated, daring herself to speak a truth that terrified her. "I was married for many years. But my husband died five years ago. I've been more or less alone since then."

Even now, so many years afterward, and in the warm gaze of Jack, this story felt unreal. A part of her still assumed she would drive home to Boston and return to the cozy embrace of her husband. A part of her would always believe that.

Jack's eyes were heavy. "Trudy, I don't know what to say. That's terrible."

Trudy filled her lungs. Normally, when people learned of her husband's death, they fell all over themselves, searching for the right way to say how sorry they were. Jack didn't do that. Instead, he touched her hand over the table and said, "I hope you know you can talk to me about it. If you want to."

This was bizarre. Ordinarily, nobody wanted to hear anything about Trudy's grief. They wanted her to shove it aside, to hide it, the way you shoved spare suitcases or boxes of decorations under the bed or in the attic.

"Thank you for saying that." Trudy filled her mouth with hot apple cider, thick with cinnamon. "Back in Boston, I completely threw myself into work to avoid dealing with my sorrow. In that way, I don't know if I ever properly healed. That said, I don't even know what it means to 'heal'." She used air quotes as Jack nodded along, his eyes glistening with empathy.

"People throw this word 'healing' around a lot," Jack said. "I heard it a lot after my parents died. I wanted to ask everyone what they meant. Where was I supposed to do all this healing? Could I buy healing somewhere? What?"

"Exactly. It seems like a commodity," Trudy said.

Trudy wondered if people like Rita were fearful of Jack's mental health because of his parents' deaths. She'd said Jack had had a hard time. It touched her heart to think he'd loved his parents so dearly.

"Some days are easier than others," Jack went on. "And other days, I'm flat on my back, wondering how to keep going."

Trudy nodded. "Wilmington has been a pretty good distraction from everything in Boston, although it's come with its own heartache."

"Your Aunt Olivia," Jack finished.

"Yes," Trudy breathed, weighing up whether or not to explain what she'd learned about Emily, Helen, and Nina. "Do you remember that photograph? The one of my Aunt Olivia, Danika, and baby Emily?"

Jack nodded, and a shadow passed over his face.

"I met Emily's daughter at the inn yesterday," Trudy went on. "Apparently, when Emily was a teenager, she gave birth to Nina. When she didn't want to marry her boyfriend, her mother, Helen, kicked her out of the house. Aunt Danika invited Emily to raise Nina at the inn."

Jack palmed the back of his neck.

"This doesn't seem like a surprise to you?"

"I've heard bits and pieces of that story," Jack admitted. "Emily isn't so much younger than I am, and I've been around Burks Falls and Wilmington all my life."

"What's Emily's mother like?"

"Helen?" Jack wrinkled his nose. "My mother used to work with her. This was after Emily moved out of the house. By this point, Helen was borderline impossible to be around, the kind of woman who put you in your place before you'd even said anything. My mother used to rant about her like nothing else. But, of course, everyone in Burks Falls and Wilmington knew how miserable she was. It was hard to hate her too much because everyone knew she hated herself most of all."

"Oh no." Trudy's heart felt bruised, remembering the beautiful smile of the young Helen in the photograph. What had happened to her? "Do you think there's any way I can bring Nina, Emily, and Helen together again? Maybe if I brought them to the inn together? Maybe if I reminded them of Danika and Olivia?"

Jack's smile was adorable yet filled with disbelief. "I don't think anyone's ever tried to bring the Mitchells back together again."

"You think it's reckless?"

"Not necessarily. I'd just step lightly if I were you."

Their burgers and fries arrived – Jack's with bacon and Trudy's with avocado and goat cheese. The fries were crispy, coated with a specialty salt that had a bite to it. As Trudy raised her burger to her lips, she was suddenly ravenous, realizing she hadn't eaten anything at all since her butter chicken. What was going on with her? It was as though her crush on Jack was the only sustenance she needed. Even now, as she gazed at him, a big slab of ketchup was across his lower lip, and a bit of cheese dotted the left side of his beard. He was still one of the most handsome men she'd ever seen.

*Oh, be careful, Trudy*, she told herself, drawing a breath. *Be careful with your silly, bruised heart.*

"You okay?" Jack asked, sensing a shift.

"I'm wonderful," Trudy admitted, pressing her lips together. "I'm better than I ever thought I would be again."

# Chapter Thirteen

Jack drove Trudy back to the Hollow's Grove Inn at eleven that night – far later than Trudy had been out since her husband's death. He was a wonderful and confident driver, his hands at six and three as he whipped down country roads. Skeletal trees burst past in blurry lines beneath the moon, and an oldies' station played hits from the seventies and eighties, many of which Jack sang quietly.

After Jack parked in front of the Hollow's Grove, they sat in the darkness of his truck in silence. They'd had hours of non-stop conversation. What was Jack thinking about now? Trudy leaned forward to peer through the front window and engage with the sharp light of the stars, which poked through the inky sky on high. She cupped her chin with her hands as Jack touched her shoulder gently. What was he going to say? Had he changed his mind about her?

"Trudy," Jack breathed, drawing her face toward his. "Can I kiss you again?"

Trudy fell into Jack's arms after that, caught in the

chaos of her swirling mind, the sparkling colors ignited by his touch and his urgent kisses. Out on the dark street of Wilmington, she felt like a teenager who'd stayed out past curfew. That said, she'd never kissed anyone as a teenager. She'd never stayed out too late because she'd never had anywhere to go.

Things were different now. It was remarkable that you could live so many different versions of one life. You could find yourself in so many alternate scenarios despite best-laid plans.

After their kiss broke, Trudy could read it in Jack's face that he wanted her to invite her upstairs. But Trudy was terrified. More than that, she didn't want to open her heart too much to him, not yet.

"I'll see you soon, I hope?"

Jack nodded. "Definitely."

Trudy hurried inside, using her enormous iron key to unlock the front door. The living room was empty, the fire was out, and the logs inside had turned to ash. Trudy went up the back staircase to her bedroom, the very same one Aunt Olivia had used as her own for the previous ten years. There, Trudy sat at the edge of her bed, cupped her knees, and wept. The onslaught of emotion from her kisses with Jack was nearly painful.

Trudy brushed her teeth, washed her face, and changed into a nightgown. In bed, she nestled her head against the pillow, reminding herself she had to wake up early to man the front desk. But her thoughts were racing. One minute, she thought of how strong Jack's hands were. Another, she considered Helen Mitchell all alone after her horrible fight with her daughter. Helen had never even met Nina nor Nina's beautiful children. For Trudy, who had no one, it all seemed like a waste.

Just after midnight, Trudy sat upright in bed. "Goodness!" She spoke aloud and reached for her notepad on the side table, where she'd listed ideas for the Hollow's Grove Inn's contribution to the Festival of Frost Floats. As Wilmington and Burks Falls businesses had begun to construct and even finalized their floats, Trudy hadn't managed to nail down a single idea that took the cake.

Not until now, anyway.

The photograph. She would center the theme around the photograph in honor of the two women who'd loved the Hollow's Grove Inn more than anything: Danika and Olivia. If Helen happened to see the photograph, too, then that couldn't hurt. Perhaps it would remind her of something. Perhaps it would remind her that forgiveness was always just around the corner if you allowed it for yourself.

After Trudy's shift the following afternoon, she showed the photograph to Frankie and explained her vision for the Christmas float.

"You could go to the Print Shop," Frankie suggested. "They print everything! Posters. Billboards. You can even get them to print photographs on a cake."

"How big do you think it should be?" Trudy asked.

"How big is the float?"

Trudy brought Frankie to the back lot of the Hollow's Grove, where she'd parked the float meant for decorating. It was approximately five feet wide and twelve feet long.

"I think you should make the photograph double-sided," Frankie said. "Five feet long and eight feet tall. After that, we can decorate the rest of the float for Christmas with trees, garlands, lights, and snowmen."

"Are you a master decorator, or what?" Trudy smiled, thrilled that Frankie wanted to help.

"Olivia always let me decorate bits and pieces of the inn," Frankie explained. "It's my passion."

"Then I'd like to pass along all decorating authority to you," Trudy said. "This inn is much more yours than mine. You've been around through thick and thin."

Frankie's cheeks were pink with embarrassment, and she pressed her palms together thoughtfully. She didn't refute what Trudy said, though. She knew, more than anyone, that she belonged there.

It occurred to Trudy that Olivia should have passed the inn on to Frankie instead of her. Then again, she was just so grateful to be in Wilmington. She couldn't question it.

Trudy headed off to speak to the owner of the print shop, a man with very thick glasses who, it turned out, happened to be Frankie's husband. Trudy cackled at the news, wondering why Frankie hadn't told her back at the inn. She assumed she'd wanted it to be a surprise.

"Frankie already called me about it," her husband, Hank, said. He looked at the photograph of Danika, Olivia, Helen, Emily, and Helen's husband for a long time as though he'd known all of them intimately. Maybe he had.

"Five by eight? Double-sided?" Hank asked.

"That's what Frankie said. She knows better than I do," Trudy assured him.

"She's been a part of my business since I started," Hank said. "I would have had to close down years ago without her help." He beamed out of loyalty and love for her and set the photograph in the copier. Trudy watched as a bright yellow light scanned over it. Immediately, the photograph found its way to the screen of Hank's computer. In this way, Trudy thought, it would exist forever. It was rather remarkable, especially because it had been hidden in an attic for who knew how long.

Hank announced he would put the print-out of the photograph on two canvases, which he would nail to a wooden structure. This rectangular structure could be easily attached to the base of the float, around which Frankie and Trudy would decorate. "Frankie said something about snowmen?" Hank said. "I don't know. When she gets involved with an art project, I know I won't see her for a while."

Trudy and Hank agreed on a price, with Trudy insisting on paying fully, without a friends and family discount. They shook on it, with Hank flashing an adorable smile. It was clear he liked a project, just like his wife.

"Oh! I almost forgot," Trudy said before she left, turning back in the doorway as the bell jangled. "I would love to have 'In Memory of Danika and Olivia' written somewhere on the photograph. Maybe above it?"

Hank looked as though he was in grave danger, as though this single ask was too much for him. "I'll add another two feet for the text to the top of the canvases. Thank goodness you thought of that before I sent it to the printer."

"Thank you. I really appreciate it," Trudy said, grateful for the care he showed his job.

With the photograph off to the printer and the real photograph safely hidden away in Trudy's purse, Trudy decided to go for a long, daydreamy stroll through Wilmington. It was five-thirty, and Christmas lights flickered around shop windows, parents led their children into restaurants hands-in-hand, and bar owners spread salt over the sidewalk in front of their establishments. Trudy recognized a few guests from the inn walking together, couples hand-in-hand. When she turned the corner near the library, her heart lifted at the sight of Nina and her family, who were peering down at the nativity scene near the courthouse. Nina's little girl reached out to touch the foot of the baby Jesus, as Nina's head shifted gently, perhaps as she explained to her daughter what the story of Jesus' birth meant for the world. Trudy could practically hear her.

Nina raised her head as though she'd sensed Trudy's gaze. Embarrassed, Trudy took a step back, but Nina had already waved her across the street, her smile warm. Optimistic after her wonderful exchange with Frankie's husband, Trudy pushed herself across the street, her heart rising in her chest as she grew closer to the little family.

"I thought that was you!" Nina cried. "I'm glad you're able to get out of the inn every once in a while."

Trudy laughed. "I have plenty of help, thankfully. It's a lot trickier to run the place than I thought it would be."

Nina nodded solemnly. "I remember. I was just a kid, but I did whatever I could to keep it up and running. Danika and Mom taught me everything – how to make the beds in that really tight and professional way, how to clean when guests are around, in a way that makes them think you're not there at all."

"She still does that at home," Nina's husband joked. "She makes the bed so tightly that I can barely get into it at night. And she sneaks up on me with the broom!"

Trudy laughed as Nina swatted her husband playfully.

"I don't believe we've been introduced," Trudy said.

"I've heard everything about you," Nina's husband said, extending his hand. "My name is Rex."

"And this is my daughter, Alexa, and my son, Dean," Nina explained, tapping their heads lovingly.

Trudy demanded they tell her everything they'd gotten up to since they'd arrived – the restaurants they'd eaten at, the small hikes along the falls, and the cakes, cocoa, and cookies they'd divulged in at the many coffee shops and cafés in the quaint town.

"Is it different than when you lived here?" Trudy asked Nina.

"A few shops and restaurants have closed down," Nina said sadly. "But the spirit of the place is still intact. I'm so grateful for that. We're raising the children in Manhattan, you know, and I sometimes wonder what they're missing."

"It must be exciting in Manhattan," Trudy offered. "I live in Boston, myself."

Nina brightened. "Beantown is a fantastic place. I did my undergrad around there before I left for medical school in New York."

"Oh!" Trudy's heartbeat quickened as she comprehended the weight of this woman's intellect. "Where did you go for your undergrad?"

"Harvard," Nina said with a soft smile.

"Wow." For a moment, Trudy was speechless. Nina was the "accidental" baby of Emily, the reason Emily and Helen no longer spoke. Yet she was perhaps the most academically impressive person Trudy had ever met. Didn't Helen want to know this person? Didn't Helen want to hold her great-grandchildren close?

"I know what she's thinking," Rex joked. "It's insane to have two children and go to medical school at the same time. But my job is really understanding, and we have help from my parents."

"I was just thinking how impressive you all are." Trudy beamed.

Nina snapped her fingers and dug around in her coat pocket. "I just remembered. Mom demanded that I get your phone number. She couldn't believe I didn't think to ask when we first met." Nina rolled her eyes playfully, proof that all mothers and daughters were caught in their own dynamic. No matter how wonderful Nina's career was, Emily would still always see her as her daughter, the little girl who needed her care.

But Trudy was surprised that Emily wanted her number. When she'd seen Emily at the restaurant, Emily had seemed resistant to the conversation, practically throwing the photograph back on the table as though it were laced with poison.

"We're inviting you over for dinner," Nina explained. "You can't say no. My mother is the best chef in the state of New York."

"You should see her say that to chefs in Manhattan," Rex joked. "They don't take kindly to it."

"They have to face the facts," Nina said proudly. "Once, Mom was a guest chef at a restaurant on the Upper West Side. Word got out quickly, and it spread like wildfire. You couldn't make reservations, and there was a line around the block. Anthony Bourdain did a whole spread about her in *Eat Magazine*."

Trudy typed her number into Nina's cell, feeling Nina's pride for her mother beaming off her. "You've convinced me," she joked. "Now that I've had Emily's cooking, I don't know how I'll go back to my microwave dinners back in Boston."

Nina winced as though the concept of microwave dinners had never even occurred to her. Probably, despite her medical school schedule back in Manhattan, she normally had home-cooked meals with her family.

"I'll text you the details later. Unfortunately, we're checking out of that magical inn tomorrow and heading to Mom's place – but we'll see you there!" Nina said.

Nina, Rex, and their children had reservations at a German restaurant down the block, where they served schnitzel, sauerkraut, soft pretzels with big chunks of salt, hearty stews, and large pints of beer. Trudy hadn't yet gone there. She wondered if Jack might want to join her there someday. She imagined them sharing two dishes and laughing about how full they were as they tried to walk it off through the snow-filled streets, touching their stomachs. She imagined their laughter echoing through Wilmington, becoming the greatest soundtrack Trudy had ever known.

# Chapter Fourteen

Due to the idiocy surrounding her accident in the grocery store parking lot, Helen was a few days late to the cemetery. As she dressed in her powder-blue dress, a pair of tights, and a sensible pair of shoes, she spoke to her husband, Brian, aloud, reminding him that she wouldn't have missed a visit with him if it hadn't been absolutely necessary.

"You know how doctors are," she said, her eyes to the mirror. "They always sit you down and make you wait your life away. It's like they don't care that you have things to do and people to see!" Helen could half-imagine Brian somewhere behind her, adjusting his tie around his neck as they prepared to go to church or attend a wedding. She could almost hear his voice, answering her, agreeing with her. Always, he'd agreed with her outwardly, even if he'd had private reservations. That was the power of their love.

Helen drove to the Burks Falls cemetery very slowly, careful not to use her right wrist too much. It embarrassed her how much it had hurt her during the night, proof she'd made a grave error in walking over that black ice. It wasn't like Helen to make mistakes.

Brian's grave was located twenty rows out and fourteen aisles from the left of the fence, situated beneath the thick arm of an oak. Beside his plot was an empty space where Helen was meant to go, which didn't necessarily scare her. In fact, she liked the idea of being able to join Brian forever, here beneath that gorgeous tree. The cemetery smelled wonderful, too, of the soft ground and the sharp cold. Had it been spring, Helen would have brought flowers or another plant, but because it was winter, she only brought herself.

Helen touched the top of the gravestone and traced her finger over the top, smiling down upon his name. "You'll never believe this," she said, speaking more formally than she had back in their bedroom. "I've broken my wrist. I felt like such a child there on the pavement, with my grocery cart flying across the parking lot. You should have seen the young grocery clerk! She looked at me as though I had three heads. I practically had to tell her the number for 9-1-1. It seems like they don't teach those sorts of things in schools anymore."

Helen waited an appropriate amount of time for Brian to answer, searching the quiet air for his deep voice. Birds twittered along the tree line, with a cardinal bucking up from the yonder maple, a sharp dash of red across the gray.

"I must have told you last week," Helen went on, "Olivia passed away. She wasn't so much older than me, you know. I can't imagine why you, Olivia, and Danika wanted to get off this planet so quickly, but here we are. You three were always so impatient."

Helen imagined Brian laughing, crow's feet drawn from his glinting eyes.

"I thought for sure they'd stop that silly festival, but it seems they're keeping it going," Helen went on. "It made me remember that very first year when Danika put us all to work to make sure it was a hit. That float you crafted was truly sensational. You carved penguins from wood! Nobody's done that since." Helen beamed at the gravestone, still in disbelief at the tremendous abilities Brian had had.

"I suppose you're wondering about Emily," Helen added regretfully, tugging at the fingers of her gloves. "She came to the hospital after my accident and insisted on driving me back to my car. I tried to get out of it, but you know how she can get. She's so stubborn." Helen swallowed the lump in her throat, remembering the way Emily's eyes had glinted with worry at Helen's wrist. It had been nice to be cared about, if only for a moment.

"I know you'd be proud of her, though," Helen continued. "That restaurant she started downtown is supposed to be sensational. It's always busy. Emily is up to her ears in top-ratings and accolades."

Overhead, a crow flew past, its black wings flapping a little too slowly. It was ominous. Helen laced her fingers together and stared intently at the grave.

"I know you think I should reach out to Emily," Helen said, her voice rasping. "But after what happened, I just don't know how, honey. Okay?" She shook her head as though what Brian demanded of her was just too much this time.

It had all happened like this.

Helen's darling, perfect, blonde-haired, blue-eyed angel daughter had returned from school one afternoon.

"I need to talk to you." Emily had placed her backpack on the ground and stood straight as a pin.

Helen stopped washing the dishes as she recognized the fear in Emily's eyes. As she dried her hands, she nodded, indicating Emily could speak.

"I don't want to apologize," Emily said. "And I don't want to say it's wrong, either. It's 1996, and times have changed for the better. We're not stuck in the fifties anymore. Women can do anything they want."

Helen frowned, at a loss. It was clear Emily had practiced this speech, perhaps in front of the mirror, but Helen wasn't making any sense of it. Had Emily gotten a bad grade in school? It was certainly possible, Helen guessed, although Emily had always had an A-average.

"It's not that I didn't know any better, either," Emily stuttered. "I'm an intelligent woman. It was a mistake, but one I will handle myself."

Helen's heartbeat intensified in her ears. "Honey, please. Stop beating around the bush!"

Emily set her jaw. "I'm pregnant."

Helen collapsed against the counter, heaving with shock. In all her years of knowing and loving Emily, she'd never imagined her to make such an enormous mistake.

"Say something, Mom," Emily demanded, her voice rasping.

Helen's heart hardened. "How?" She shook her head, searching for words. "How could you, Emily Mitchell of all people, let this happen?"

Emily's eyes were red with anger and fear. "How do you think it happened, Momma?"

Helen flared her nostrils. Never in her life had Emily spoken to Helen like this. She'd taught her to be more responsible, hadn't she? She'd taught her to respect her elders.

Helen turned away from Emily and continued to do the dishes, drawing suds over the plates and scrubbing hard with her nails. She could feel Emily behind her, her eyes boring into her back. When she turned off the water, Helen heard herself say, "Who is the father?"

Emily coughed. "Everett Proctor."

Helen's heart opened the slightest bit. She turned to give Emily a half-smile. "He's a remarkable young man."

It was true. Everett was the second-smartest kid in school after Emily. He was class president, captain of the football team, and a summertime manager at the Country Club, where Helen and Brian played golf and went to the pool. Over the years, Helen had suggested to Emily that she should hang around with that Proctor boy more often, that he was clearly going places, the same as she was.

Now, the stars had aligned. It had happened slightly too early, of course, as Emily was only sixteen years old. But this meant that the Proctor and Mitchell families would be united forever. This meant Helen's grandchild would have unrivaled intellect and beauty across all of Burks Falls and Wilmington.

"And what did Everett say when you told him?" Helen asked.

Emily set her jaw. "I haven't told him."

Helen's smile fell. "He needs to know, honey. He's going to be a father. That's a big thing for a young man to wrap his mind around."

"He's not the one who has to give birth," Emily pointed out.

Helen tried to smile again, but she was finding it increasingly difficult. "But he's going to be a husband and a father. He has a great deal of responsibility to take on. He's just a sixteen-year-old boy, honey."

"He's not going to be a husband," Emily interjected.

Helen's mouth went dry. "Beg your pardon?"

Emily crossed her arms over her chest, looking as resolute as she had when she'd won the town spelling bee. "I'm not going to marry Everett Proctor."

"But honey. You're having his baby. You're going to have a family."

"I'm not going to stay in Burks Falls forever, Mom," Emily explained stiffly. "I've told you over and over again. I want to go to culinary school. I have dreams."

"But you're pregnant," Helen repeated. "I know it's not especially feminist to say so, but that changes everything."

"It's not going to change everything for me," Emily insisted. "I can do this. I can care for the baby by myself, and I can go to culinary school. I can do it all."

"You can't," Helen insisted. Anger boiled over in her tone, and she felt on the verge of screaming. What would the entire town say if Emily refused to marry Everett Proctor? What would they think of Helen for raising a young woman like that? Oh, she imagined walking through the grocery store, listening to everyone gossip about what a horrible mother she was. Maybe Brian would even blame her for this – thinking of her as a terrible role model. What would she do?

Before Helen could beg Emily to listen to reason, Emily spun on her heel and ran to her bedroom, where she slammed the door. She turned on her speakers so that the door vibrated. Helen knelt on the floor and sobbed into her thighs for what felt like hours until Brian found her there, blubbering. When she explained Emily's predicament, along with Emily's decision never to marry Everett, Brian's cheeks turned cherry red— and he stomped to Emily's bedroom and knocked on the door. The anger he spewed at her made Helen shiver and hide herself away in the bedroom. She didn't want to hear exactly what he said to her, but she hoped whatever he uttered forced Emily to do exactly what was right.

The remaining dishes sat in the sink for the rest of the night. Nobody ate dinner. And when Brian returned to the bedroom later on, he was ashen and clearly at a loss. Nothing he'd said had made a dent in Emily's mission.

For many days, Helen and Brian didn't speak to Emily. Helen expected Emily to come around and to recognize the error in her thinking. But a week after Emily's announcement, she made another, informing Helen she was going to live with her Aunt Danika at the Hollow's Grove Inn. Beside her were two suitcases, packed with everything she supposedly needed. Helen was too stunned to insist she stay. She remained silent as Emily burst out the front door and walked toward the bus stop, her chin raised. For the tenth time that week, Helen fell to the floor to sob.

Danika answered the Hollow's Grove phone on the third ring.

"Good afternoon! This is the Hollow's Grove Inn, Danika speaking."

"How dare you?" Helen blared, sounding like a crazy woman in a film.

Danika's tone shifted, and she whispered, "Helen, this isn't the time."

"This is the time because I say it's the time," Helen shot back. "We need Emily here. We need to help her through this."

"You think you know what Emily needs," Danika began.

"I don't just think," Helen said. "I'm her mother. I raised her. You never had children. You can't possibly understand."

Danika remained quiet on the other line. Helen knew she'd struck her where it hurt the most— reminding Danika that she'd never gotten married, never settled down, and never had a baby. Danika had wanted it so desperately. It was anyone's guess why it hadn't turned out, although people across Burks Falls and Wilmington gossiped that Danika's only true love had abandoned her immediately after proposing, breaking her heart in the process. She'd never recovered.

"If you're willing to listen to Emily and what she needs, then you're welcome to come to the inn any time to discuss it," Danika said coldly. "If your plan is to come to the inn and yell at her until she marries that Everett kid, then you're not welcome here."

"A baby needs both parents!" Helen said.

"And Emily needs to have the life she deserves," Danika said.

"This is a mistake. Tell me you understand that," Helen begged.

"I love Emily," Danika said. "I won't let anything happen to her. And I'm going to help her every step of the way, with your help or without it." Then, she hung up.

Helen explained Emily's decision to Brian that night. Her husband's face was very pale and sagging, as he said Emily would surely get over it. "She'll be back in three months. Mark my words."

But Emily did not come back. As time went on, Helen and Brian's lives became very quiet, edged with sorrow. Frequently, they ate in front of the television, unable to speak to one another. Helen wasn't sure if they blamed one another for what had befallen Emily or if they hated one another for pushing Emily out of the house. There was torment in Brian's eyes, and he hardly kissed her anymore, his touch lingering for only a second after a hug. Helen had begun to feel desperately lonely, walking around their family home without anything to do. She'd considered getting a job, something to fill her time, somewhere to put her anxious thoughts. It was true what Emily had said; *it was the nineties, and women did all sorts of jobs.*

Meanwhile, in Wilmington, Helen knew that Emily, Danika, and Danika's best friend, Olivia, had built a wonderful universe together. Danika and Olivia had always been far more creative than Helen; they'd always laughed longer and been more intellectual. Emily had gotten along with them marvelously and had frequently spent the night at the Hollow's Grove, even before the pregnancy. Now, Emily never returned to her boring, old mother and father. She'd never needed them.

In one fell swoop, Helen had lost her daughter, her sister, and her friend, Olivia. It often kept her awake at night, staring through the darkness. She imagined herself getting into her car and driving to the neighboring town, where she would sit near the fireplace of the Hollow's Grove and hold her daughter's hand. She imagined Emily telling her about how sick she felt during pregnancy; she imagined Emily listing out the names she wanted to give the baby.

Remarkably, Emily had changed schools, transferring from Burks Falls to Wilmington. With that switch, she'd somehow avoided telling anyone that her baby was

Everett Proctor's. According to local gossip that Helen gleaned at the hair salon, Everett was now dating one of the cheerleaders from Burks Falls, none the wiser that Emily was pregnant with his child. Helen considered going over to the Proctor family home and telling them everything. But what good would that do? It would only alienate Emily more. Besides, the Proctors would probably hate Helen for altering the course of Everett's life. In their eyes, he was set to go to the city and do great things, whatever that meant.

Approximately nine months after Emily's pregnancy announcement, Helen and Brian were seated in the shadows of the living room, watching a talk show. The phone rang at an ungodly hour, long after it was appropriate to call. Helen and Brian locked eyes across the room. Both were thinking the same thing. Neither was up to the task of saying it aloud.

Finally, Brian burst up from his chair and hurried to the phone. Gasping for breath, he answered it. "Hello? Mitchell residence?"

Helen sat at the edge of her seat, listening.

"Is that so?" Brian's voice softened. "Wow. I really can't believe this."

Helen stood up and inched toward him.

"Yes. I can't imagine not being there," Brian breathed, his shoulders shaking. "I'll see you soon, honey. Okay? I love you."

Slowly, Brian placed the phone in the cradle and turned to gaze at Helen through the dark kitchen. His eyes were red.

"That was Emily," he said. "She's in labor. And she wants us there."

Helen's knees knocked together with panic. All these

months, she and Brian had stood by what they'd said, assured they'd been in the right. But what if they hadn't been? What if what Emily wanted was the only correct course?

"You want to go?" Helen breathed.

Brian stepped toward her and reached out to take her hand. "I know I've been very hard on her."

Helen nodded. She had been, too.

"But this is our grandchild, Helen," he continued, his words syncopated. "I wouldn't miss this for the world."

* * *

As Helen sat in the cemetery, reflecting on the past, the snowfall thickened, drawing a blanket of white over Brian's grave. The tears on her cheeks froze immediately, and she reached up to touch the crepe-paper skin of her face. She hadn't realized she'd been crying. As she stared at Brian's grave, her head heavy with memories, she imagined Brian telling her to get home. "The roads will be bad soon," he said earnestly. "You have to be careful with that wrist."

Helen kissed the fingers of her glove and pressed them against the top of the grave, telling Brian quietly that she would be there again next week and the one after that. She never wanted him to feel as alone as she did. She wouldn't have wished that on her worst enemy.

# Chapter Fifteen

Nina and Emily didn't wait to invite Trudy for dinner. A text dinged in mere hours after Trudy had given Nina her number, asking if she could make it tomorrow for a "five-course meal." Trudy soon found herself in a group chat with Nina and Emily, her cheeks hot with excitement. The only group chats she'd been invited to had long-ago died out or else had had something to do with her coffeeshop franchise. This felt like something special.

TRUDY: You know, Emily, we can always order pizza or something. You don't have to cook every day of the week!

EMILY: Don't be silly. I would never trust anyone else in the kitchen.

NINA: She's not lying. That's the reason I'm such a bad cook. My mother never wanted to let me near her cookware!

EMILY: You're not bad, Nina.

EMILY: It's just good you found the medical profession instead.

NINA: Mom!

Trudy laughed into her phone, cradling it as she leaned against the counter of the Hollow's Grove, wishing guests goodnight as they breezed past, removing their scarves and shaking snow from their curls.

"You look happy," Max, the server from the dining room, said as he hurried by.

"There's something about this place," Trudy explained, pocketing the phone. "Oh! Hey. Max. I have a question for you."

Max's eyes spun with curiosity.

"Would you be willing to help Frankie and me with the Christmas float this year?"

"Frankie has already recruited me," Max said proudly. "I've helped the past three years. Olivia always counted on me to carry the heavier items onto the float. One year, I had to haul a statue of a horse on there. It must have weighed two-hundred pounds."

Trudy cackled. "You're kidding! What was the theme?"

"Olivia loved that book, *Black Beauty*," Max remembered. "She painted the statue black and wore a beautiful old riding outfit. If I remember correctly, the rest of the float was decorated with Christmas trees and snowmen, so it looked like she rode the horse through a winter wonderland."

"Wow." Trudy struggled to align this picture with Aunt Olivia, who'd supposedly died without many friends.

"Are you going to dress up for the festival?" Max asked.

"I think I'll let the float speak for itself," Trudy said.

That night before Trudy went to sleep, she nestled under the sheets with her curls splayed across the pillows and searched her mind for the perfect thing to text Jack. All day, they'd written back and forth, with Jack explaining the Christmas tree farm was in a state of "Christmas chaos." Apparently, many families had waited quite a long time to buy their tree, and parents were bickering over which to purchase.

JACK: It's getting crazy around here. One mother said Christmas was ruined.

TRUDY: All because of a tree?

JACK: You know how people get around the holidays. Everything has to be perfect. And when it isn't...

TRUDY: Everything falls apart. I know.

Actually, Trudy didn't fully understand that. Back when she'd been a kid, her mother had given her the toys from the local toy drive and left her alone all day to play with them. At school, other children had talked about what they wanted to ask Santa for Christmas, and Trudy had understood that Santa didn't pay attention to her wishes. For a while, she'd assumed she was just a naughty kid.

TRUDY: I hope everyone still has their fingers, toys, and spouses at the Christmas tree farm.

JACK: Ha. In the end, everyone went home safe and happy.

JACK: I'm exhausted! I think I chopped down twenty-eight trees today.

TRUDY: Paul Bunyan strikes again!

Over the next full hour, long past Trudy's bedtime, she and Jack exchanged flirtatious text messages, drawing Trudy further and further from sleep.

JACK: Did you realize it's midnight?

TRUDY: Oh no!

Trudy laughed with wonder. It felt as though they'd traveled through time.

JACK: I'd better hit the hay. See you soon, I hope?

TRUDY: I have plans tomorrow, but the next day, I'm free as a bird.

JACK: Great. I want to take you out to dinner.

TRUDY: I heard about this German restaurant downtown.

JACK: It's delicious. Let's do it.

* * *

Frankie appeared at the front desk the following day at four-thirty, right on time as always, and announced that Hank's printouts for the float were completed. "He's going to drop the structure off this evening. I'll have Max attach it to the float so that we can get started on the decorations after that."

"Have you seen it?" Trudy asked, nervous that the photograph had turned out grainy.

"It looks really good," Frankie said somberly. "I told you. Hank is the best."

Trudy floated through her tasks after that, retreating upstairs to change into a dark green dress and a pair of flats. She ran a brush through her hair and assessed her reflection, marveling at her own nerves. The dinner with Nina and Emily felt like a first step toward something. She felt more in-tune with Olivia than ever.

Emily's house was located on the outskirts of Burks Falls, not far from the Christmas tree farm, at the edge of a sprawling lawn peppered with huge oaks, maples, and willow trees. The structure itself was proof of Emily's status in the restaurant industry: a full three stories, with a pool and hot tub outside and a foyer with cathedral-like ceilings. Emily and Nina beckoned Trudy into the warmth, taking her coat and fretting over her.

"I hope the drive wasn't too bad. I sometimes hate that we live out here in the boonies," Emily said.

"It was just fine," Trudy assured her. "It's a gorgeous property. Have you been here long?"

"My husband, Nina, and I moved in about fifteen years ago," Emily explained, guiding Trudy into the living room, where a dramatic stone fireplace filled most of the wall, and a fire crackled through lumber. A bottle of wine sat on the coffee table in front of a leather couch.

As Nina poured Trudy a glass, Trudy asked, "Is the rest of your family joining us tonight?"

"My husband, Rex, and the kids are going out to eat,"

Emily explained. "So, it's just us girls. I hope that's okay?"

"Of course!" Trudy was touched that Emily and Nina wanted private time with her. She assumed this was what it felt like to be a part of a real family, sequestering off with the other women to tell secrets from the past.

"I hope you like French food," Emily said. "I recently went on an exploratory trip through Aix-en-Provence and got some inspiration."

"It sounds like there's no cuisine you're afraid to tackle," Trudy said.

"Sometimes, I feel limited by the Italian restaurant," Emily admitted.

"Tell me," Trudy said, not wanting to be nosy but eager to learn, "when did you go to culinary school?"

"I was twenty when I started," Emily said. "Which meant that Nina here was three."

"That must have been very difficult," Trudy offered.

"You know what? Everyone told me it would be hard," Emily said thoughtfully. "But I had so much help. As Nina already explained to you, we'd been living at the Hollow's Grove for quite a while by then, and Nina fit in easily with the staff and with Danika and Olivia. I was able to do the long nights required of me in culinary school, and I knew someone was always eager to help out with Nina." Emily smiled tenderly at her daughter.

"Eventually, we moved out of the Hollow's Grove," Emily went on. "I graduated from culinary school and took a job in Providence for a while. That's where I really got my skills, I think."

"That's where she met Kurt," Nina explained with a smile.

"My husband," Emily said. "When I told him I

wanted to come up here to be closer to family, he didn't hesitate. He even suggested I open my own restaurant. He operates the business, and I focus on the food."

"Yin and yang," Trudy suggested, and Nina and Emily laughed.

"You know," Emily began, leaning back, "When I met you at the Hollow's Grove after your aunt's funeral, I realized I hadn't been there in many years. I'd avoided it, more or less, after Aunt Danika died."

Nina's eyes were wounded. "It was so sudden. Aunt Danika had always been a portrait of health."

"Always forcing us to take our vitamins and get enough exercise," Emily affirmed, her eyes wet. "I feel like I never really let her know how much she meant to me, you know? She stepped in when everything in my life was falling apart."

From the kitchen, a beeper sounded. Emily jumped to her feet and hurried out. "Appetizer in three minutes! Get ready!" Behind her words was the tang of her own sorrow.

Nina adjusted her blonde curls behind her ears. "It means a lot that you're here," she said softly. "I think Mom beats herself up for not going to see Olivia more often. The truth is, going to the inn was just so painful for us after Danika. Aunt Danika even tried to pass the inn down to one of us, but Mom didn't want anything to do with it. That's why Olivia had to take over in the first place."

Trudy sipped her wine contemplatively. If there was anything she understood, it was the wounds of the past, which so often never seemed to heal.

The first appetizer was an Alsatian cheese tart: both creamy and smoky at once, sprinkled with sharp and tangy pieces of bacon. Trudy allowed herself to fall into the inviting flavors, reminding herself, yet again, of her microwave dinners back in Boston. Could she really return to them? And how would Jack work into all of that?

"How did you meet Jack, by the way?" It was as though Emily had read her mind.

"Jack? Jack, who?" Nina asked.

"You know," Emily gave her a warning smile. "Jack Carter."

"Oh! That Jack." Nina winced.

"He delivered twenty-five Christmas trees to the inn on my first day," Trudy said, unable to hide the excitement in her voice. "Ever since then, we've been hanging out a little bit. He helped me decorate the inn for Christmas." She felt her cheeks grow warm.

Both Nina and Emily peered at her curiously. Trudy chewed and swallowed another bite of cheese tart, daring herself to ask the question she knew she needed to.

"Burks Falls and Wilmington seem to handle Jack like he's breakable," Trudy admitted. "Rita at the bar warned me to watch out for his feelings. Do either of you know why?"

Emily and Nina exchanged worried glances. At that moment, Trudy thought of every possible thing that could go wrong. Maybe Jack was a serial killer. Maybe Jack was a wild gambling addict. Maybe Jack was secretly married.

Emily cleared her throat. "Jack was engaged to my best friend for many years. Allegra."

Trudy's heartbeat thudded. She tried not to betray any emotion. "What happened between them?"

"Allegra took off," Emily said with a shrug. "This was about a year ago, I guess. We went out to dinner the night before, and she told me she was having second thoughts about marrying Jack. I told her she was crazy. Jack and Allegra had been together for seven years at that point. Nobody thought they were anything but perfect for each other. And then, whoosh." Emily snapped her fingers. "She was gone."

"And you never heard from her, either?" Trudy was heavy with disbelief.

"She texted me about six months ago," Emily said. "She apologized for leaving like that, but she also never told me where she'd gone or what she was up to. I felt betrayed. But I also felt really bad for Jack. He'd given her everything, you know? All year, his eyes have been so empty." Emily pressed her lips together. "Until I saw him the other day at my restaurant."

Trudy tilted her head with confusion.

"The way he looked at you," Emily explained. "It made him look the way he used to. He looked lighter and happier than I'd seen him in ages. I guess that's why both towns are nervous about you, Trudy. They see the way Jack looks at you, and they don't want him to get hurt again."

Trudy replied. "I never want to hurt Jack. I don't know how I ever could."

"People hurt people," Emily said sadly, her eyes to the window, where snow peppered the darkness. "Even when we don't plan to."

Trudy knew Emily was speaking about her mother, Danika, and Olivia and all the tremendous pain the Mitchell and Potter family had taken on in the previous decades. But before she could pry Emily for more details about her mother, about whether or not they could ever mend their relationship, another beeper sounded from the kitchen. Emily sprung up, wiping tears from her cheeks as she went. Now wasn't the time for such probing questions. Now was the time to sit in the warmth of their familial love, to eat to their hearts' content, and prepare themselves for Christmas.

One thing was clear: both Nina and Emily wanted to get to know Trudy. And, in the wake of her Aunt Olivia's death, Trudy's heart was much more open to being known. It was truly extraordinary – and terrifying. Trudy had forgotten what it meant to be really and truly known and understood. She'd allowed the concept to be buried away with her husband. Yet here it was again, electrifying her in the warmth of Emily and Nina's smiles.

# Chapter Sixteen

Trudy returned to the Hollow's Grove Inn at ten-thirty that night, her stomach straining against the waistband of her jeans. Most of the guest room lights were out, and the fire embers were dying in the hearth. Frankie yawned from behind the front desk, adjusting her enormous glasses over her nose.

"You should head home, Frankie."

"Not before I show you this. Follow me!"

Frankie tugged her coat over her shoulders and led Trudy to the lot behind the inn. "Max worked his little heart out tonight," she explained as she opened the back door and hurried through the snow to remove a large tarp over the Christmas float.

Just as Frankie had promised, Max had connected the enormous, double-sided photograph to the float. Now, even taller than they'd been in life, Danika, Olivia, Helen, and Helen's husband smiled out at them, with the words: IN MEMORY OF DANIKA AND OLIVIA written in dramatic cursive lettering at the top. Trudy's heart flipped over.

"It looks even better than I imagined," she breathed.

Frankie beamed. "Hank's proud of it, too." Frankie continued to explain her plans for tomorrow's decorating, which would require Trudy's helping hand, and Trudy nodded along, eyes to Aunt Olivia's in the photograph. She hoped she was doing the right thing.

From the window of the inn, Trudy watched as Frankie started her car and maneuvered through the dark, her bright lights flashing against tree trunks. When Frankie disappeared around the corner, Trudy put another log in the fire and rubbed her palms together, no longer tired in the least. A memory had begun to tug at her, drawing up from the back caverns of her mind. She hadn't thought of it in years.

She'd been seventeen at the time. If memory served her correctly, she'd been studying for the GED, bent on never returning to school and pursuing a separate path in life, one that had nothing to do with football games and report cards filled with As. Aunt Olivia had been kind about her mission, sensing the ways in which Trudy would never fit into an ordinary high school. Even with new, clean clothes on, she couldn't shake the feeling that she was a kid from poverty. All the other teenagers saw it, too – as though her malnutrition showed in her teeth or her skinny arms.

It was Christmas, a holiday season Trudy still hadn't learned to care much about. She hadn't heard from her mother in a year and a half at that point and frequently spent hours thinking about her, about where she'd ended up and if she was okay. She was reading a biology textbook about genetics, about how much of her looks and her personality was taken directly from her mother. It seemed unlikely that she would ever outgrow anything her mother had been. When she expressed these feelings to Aunt Olivia, Aunt Olivia said only: "But you owe it to yourself to try."

Trudy took a break from biology to make a slice of toast in the kitchen. This was long before Olivia's move to the Hollow's Grove and many years after her husband, Matt had left her. Even still, there were traces of Matt around the house: a large sheepskin coat that couldn't have fit Olivia, men's shampoo, and a dog leash that Trudy suspected had belonged to Matt's dog. It wasn't clear to Trudy why Matt had left Olivia. Because Trudy was terrible at communication, she wasn't sure she would ever find out.

The kitchen was connected to the front room, where Aunt Olivia often sat to read and watch the snow. It was there she'd set up and decorated the Christmas tree with garlands and popcorn and photographs of her parents, both of whom had died long ago. Although Trudy didn't spend much time in that room, she secretly considered the tree to be extremely beautiful. Olivia had a real eye for detail.

As Trudy placed the toast into the toaster, she heard a muffled sob followed by a whispered voice. The voice was clearly Danika's, her aunt's best friend. That meant the sobbing came from Olivia. So as not to be heard, she didn't lower the toast into the toaster and shifted slowly across the kitchen, craning to hear.

"I just can't help but think," Aunt Olivia whispered through tears, "that none of it mattered."

Trudy stopped at the edge of the kitchen and gingerly peered around the doorframe. She knew spying was wrong— but she burned with the desire to know something more about her aunt. Something that she couldn't find out with their stunted conversations and Aunt Olivia's urgings to keep working on her GED.

"Don't say that," Danika said, touching Olivia's shoulder gently.

"Don't you think it, too?" Olivia asked, gasping for breath. "By now, I thought my life would be so different. I thought Matt and I would have at least four children. That I'd have some kind of direction by now."

"Honey, you do have direction," Danika reminded her.

Olivia rubbed her chest hard, trying to steady her breathing. "I just wish he hadn't sent me the letter. I was happy to pretend he'd never existed at all."

"The man never had a lot of empathy," Danika offered. "Or intellect."

Olivia snorted through tears and raised a photograph through the dark shadows. "She's a cute baby. I'll give her that."

"All babies are cute," Danika said. "This one was unlucky enough to be born Matt's daughter."

Olivia's chin wiggled as she tried to suppress her tears. "I've tried to throw away all my feelings for Matt. I've put all my efforts into Trudy. Into my hopes for her. But that doesn't feel like it's going anywhere, either."

"You're so patient with her," Danika assured her. "Which is all you can be. You said it yourself. You don't have a clear picture of what it was like to grow up the way she did. She never had enough to eat, never had clean clothes to wear."

Olivia rubbed her temples. "I wish I could have figured out where they were sooner. It breaks me up inside, thinking I could have done something."

"You couldn't have," Danika said.

"I can't believe she even agreed to the GED," Olivia whispered.

"It's proof you're getting through to her. It's happening very slowly. But that's how these sorts of transformations go."

Olivia sniffed. "She's been a blessing in my life. I might have floated away without her."

"I wouldn't have let you float away," Danika said. "Don't you remember what I told you? You can get rid of this house whenever you want to and come live with me at the Hollow's Grove."

"Not now," Olivia said quietly. "It's Trudy's home. She needs solid ground right now."

"If and when she goes to college," Danika affirmed. "That's when you're coming. There's no use to being alone in this life. I genuinely believe that's why we met each other."

Olivia closed her eyes, and the lights from the Christmas tree illuminated her eyelids with reds and greens. "Thank you for listening to me cry all night." She tried to laugh, but her smile fell off her face.

"That's what I'm here for," Danika assured her. "I can't count how many times you've done the same for me."

* * *

Trudy met Ben at The Lucky Bean. She was in her late twenties at the time, a new franchise owner, and up to her ears in stress. Every morning, she went for a long jog through Boston, repeating mantras to herself as she kept up a steady rhythm. She had to make it. She had to become the woman she'd always dreamed of becoming. She could not fall back into poverty.

Ben was one of those early-internet-age workers, always with a laptop in the corner of a coffee shop as he wrote blogs, copy, and the occasional screenplay for local commercials. For whatever reason, on that day, his normal coffee shop's Wi-Fi was down, and he'd decided to try out the new place down the block.

Just as Ben approached the counter, the espresso machine let out a high-pitched scream and immediately shut down. Trudy's barista, a nineteen-year-old with ironic tattoos of Pop-Eye the Sailor, stabbed buttons on the espresso machine, demanding it come back to life. The line behind Ben began to lengthen until the people who entered turned right around in retreat.

Trudy had been working in the coffee industry for many years at that point, and her initial instinct was to call a repairman. Ben interjected, his puppy-dog eyes widening as he explained that he knew his way around machinery. Could he help?

Trudy was resistant. She didn't know this guy. What if he broke the machine? Worse: what if he lost one of his fingers in the process? But the line of customers was growing weary, and she was terrified that they would tell their friends and friends of friends about their horrific encounter at The Lucky Bean. The first few days of every new franchise opening were essential.

Lucky for Trudy, Ben didn't need long with the machine. He tinkered and poked and pressed buttons, and very soon, he slotted another helping of fresh beans into the sterling silver and ground them. The familiar and welcoming smell of coffee filled the air. Trudy realized she hadn't breathed fully since it had broken down. She now inhaled.

Trudy made Ben a gorgeous double-shot mocha with whipped cream as a thank you and brought it to his table. He was already set up with his computer, his fingers flying over the keys. She allowed herself to consider how handsome he was, with his floppy black hair and his smooth, slightly chubby cheeks. She even allowed herself to remember how long it had been since she'd gone out on a date— three years? Maybe four?

"That is a lot of whipped cream!" Ben laughed, and dimples formed on his cheeks.

"I can't thank you enough," Trudy said, blushing. "This is my fourth location for The Lucky Bean. You'd think I'd know my way around repairing a machine at this point."

Ben tilted his head, considering her, his expression filled with intrigue. Trudy couldn't imagine what that meant. Was there a spot of food on her face?

"Maybe I could give you a few pointers?" Ben suggested.

Trudy's heartbeat intensified. "Oh, that's okay. It's not your problem."

"I'd really like to," Ben said. "The shop closes at seven, yeah? I'll be done with work by then."

Trudy glanced momentarily at the script he had up on his computer, where she read:

**INTERIOR: BALLROOM AT NIGHT**

She'd never met anyone who'd written scripts before.

"All right," Trudy said. "But I'll have to make you another double-shot, whipped mocha to thank you."

"Maybe you can just buy me a drink," Ben suggested. "There's a great bar down the street."

Trudy nearly fell to her knees.

That night, after the coffee shop cleared out to leave only Trudy and Ben, Ben packed up his laptop, his books, and his notebook and strode toward Trudy at the counter, where she clutched a wet rag nervously.

"I have to confess something," he said.

"Okay?"

"I had no idea what I was doing with that machine," he said. "The fact that it started up again is a complete mystery to me."

Trudy's smile burst open.

"I hope you'll still consider going out for a drink with me," Ben continued. "But I've been sitting over there, sweating all evening, wondering how I could possibly tell you I'd lied."

"That's a pretty big lie, sir," Trudy said, crossing her arms over her chest. "I might need you to buy me that drink instead of the other way around. Just to make up for it."

It occurred to Trudy that this was always how she'd imagined meeting her partner: in a coffee shop as the blue light of the evening dimmed through the wide windows, casting a ghoulish aura across the empty tables. She wanted to fall in love with him instantly. Instead, she fell in love with him about two weeks after that.

Trudy and Ben had a wedding of fifty people, mostly Ben's friends and family, plus those Trudy was closest to from The Lucky Bean. Trudy also invited Aunt Olivia, the woman who'd taken her in at sixteen, pushed her to take the GED, and sent her monthly checks to ensure she was able to eat and sustain herself during university. Aunt Olivia sent her RSVP first— a resounding YES.

Olivia sat in the second row of the church, one of the

few on Trudy's side. She wore a sleek pink dress with ruffled sleeves and high heels, and her hair was a rush of dark blonde curls. Trudy had a hunch she'd recently dyed her hair, opting for a fresh look in her fifties. By that time, she'd moved into the Hollow's Grove to help Danika with the inn, shelling off years of loneliness in pursuit of family and companionship.

After the ceremony, Trudy found Aunt Olivia in the small crowd outside the church. She threw her arms around her and shivered in the older woman's embrace. The emotional highs of the day were almost too much to bear.

"Oh, honey," Aunt Olivia breathed. "You look gorgeous."

"So do you." Trudy laughed as their hug broke, but she kept her hands on Aunt Olivia's shoulders.

"You know," Olivia began thoughtfully, "I think that might be the first time you've really hugged me."

Trudy's throat tightened with surprise. Olivia's point was not made in malice— but it did point clearly to the fact of Trudy's healing. As a teenager, she hadn't allowed anyone to touch her. She hadn't known how to accept love. Here and now, minutes after her marriage to Ben and in the warm embrace of Aunt Olivia, she was reminded of that timid, black-hearted teenage girl she'd once been.

"Thank you for everything," Trudy whispered. "I never would have made it here without you."

Olivia squeezed both of her hands. "You would have made it. You're a wildly intelligent young woman. I was just pleased to have any involvement in your life at all."

"Ben and I will come to Wilmington soon," Trudy promised, even as the idea of returning filled her with a sense of dread – as though a previous version of herself lurked in the shadows, ready to tear her back down. "It's time."

"Don't worry yourself too much," Olivia said. "I know you're working hard here in Boston. How many coffee shops have you opened now?" She laughed gently. "We'll see each other when we see each other. If that's in one year or three years, I'll be happy. I'm just thrilled I got to see you on this special day."

Ben appeared after that, swallowing Aunt Olivia with a hug as he promised her he'd be by Trudy's side in all things, that he'd love her harder than he'd ever loved a soul. Trudy hadn't once considered this wouldn't be possible. It had seemed as factual as that biology textbook from high school, as firm as any law of gravity.

# Chapter Seventeen

The next several days were a flurry of activity at the Hollow's Grove. With Frankie at the helm, Trudy, Frankie, Max, and several other staff members worked tirelessly on the float, stringing lights, securing plastic snowmen, reindeer, and a Santa Claus to the base, setting up a speaker system to play Christmas songs, and covering the entire thing with heaps of fake snow. They finished it with three days to spare, dusting off their hands as they gazed up at their creation— a testament to Danika and Olivia's love for the Festival of Frost Floats, their love for the inn, and their love for each other. As far as Trudy was concerned, theirs was a friendship that outpaced many marriage partnerships. They'd been there for one another through heartache and loneliness, through raising Trudy, Emily, and even Nina. The festival needed to reflect that.

"Not bad," Frankie said under her breath as she assessed the final iteration of the float. She grabbed her phone from her pocket and took several shots, explaining she wanted to show Hank their hard work. "He loves being featured in the Festival of Frost Floats. This is the fourth time people have used his services. Maybe fifth."

Trudy took a photograph, too. Her cheeks were warm after throwing buckets of fake snow and securing portions of it with a hammer and a nail. The hammer was now hanging at her side, a bit of fluff stuck to the head. From the back door, someone called Max's name, saying they needed him in the dining room pronto.

"I better get back to the front desk," Frankie said, sounding authoritative and strong. "Help me put the tarp back on?"

As Trudy and Frankie pulled the protective tarp back over the float, Trudy bubbled with anticipation. The next time they unfurled the tarp would be the day of the festival. It was nearly time.

With Frankie behind the front desk, the float finished for the parade, and a bright blue sky arcing overhead, Trudy was too effervescent to do anything but leap in her car, turn on the oldies' radio station, and drive over to the Christmas tree farm. As she went, she slowed several times to analyze the other Christmas floats parked along side streets. Most featured wonderful themes— Christmas cowboys, the movie *Frozen*, *Star Wars*, and Christmas Elvis. As she drove, she received a phone call with final confirmation for yet another food truck she'd hired for the festival, where guests could order everything from tacos to burgers to baked goods. Expectation for the festival brimmed across Wilmington, with businesses posting signs out in front of their windows saying: SEE YOU ON THE 23rd!

Ten cars were parked at the Christmas tree farm, more than Trudy had seen in a few days. It struck her as funny yet marvellously so that she'd spent so much of her time lately at the farm, walking hand-in-hand with Jack, strolling through the trees and occasionally kissing, sneaking around as though they were teenagers.

As she got out of her car, Murphy, one of Jack's employees, secured a Christmas tree on someone's truck and waved.

"We've got an uptick in sales," he explained as he headed over to her. "Everyone needs extra trees for their Christmas floats."

"That's wonderful!"

Murphy nodded and palmed the back of his neck, his eyes flickering. Trudy hadn't spoken to him often. Was he always so anxious?

"Does Jack know you're stopping by?"

"No," Trudy said. "This is a spontaneous visit. Where can I find him?"

Murphy glanced toward the shack, where two other boys spoke with visitors, directing them to different areas of the Christmas tree farm based on their needs.

"Maybe you should come back another time," Murphy suggested. "We're pretty busy."

"It's not that bad," Trudy said. "If Jack's with a customer, I can just wait in the shack." This was something she'd done before. As she'd sat, she'd had to listen to an employee's favorite podcast about the science of animals. That one had been about gerbils.

Murphy took a hesitant step toward the shack. Why was he acting so strangely? Trudy scanned the parking lot and noted that Jack's truck was parked, as was the larger truck he used for deliveries. He had to be around there somewhere.

But suddenly, there was a flash of something bright between the trees. Murphy's face was stricken, and Trudy followed his gaze toward that light, where a very blonde woman stepped out from behind a line of trees. She wore a powder pink coat and a fuzzy headband, and she was slender with long, twiggy legs. Her face was stoic, and she nodded at something the man beside her said.

Trudy's heart dropped into her stomach. The man was Jack – and he looked very serious, as though whatever they discussed was a matter of life and death.

Trudy's thoughts raced for an explanation. Perhaps that woman was a customer hungry for top tips on Christmas tree watering. Jack took his work very seriously. Or perhaps she'd lost her child somewhere on the farm, and Jack was assuring her they'd find him. Perhaps.

But the look on Murphy's face told Trudy everything she needed to know. That woman wasn't just any woman. She wasn't a customer, either. And it was suddenly, breathlessly clear that Trudy needed to get as far away from the Christmas tree farm as she could. Immediately.

"I'd better get going," Trudy said, her voice breaking. She considered making an excuse, but nothing came to her mind. "Thanks for your help, Murphy."

Before Murphy could respond, Trudy dropped herself into the car, shut the door, cranked the engine, and whipped out of there. Her heart blasted again and again in her throat, and the world around her blurred with the white of the snow, the brown of the line of trees, and the sharp blue of the sky. For a long time, she drove like that, unable to breathe, as tears traced down her cheeks. When she reached a gas station near the highway, she yanked into a parking spot and placed her forehead against the steering wheel. What had she been thinking? Why had she assumed she and Jack were falling in love?

Before she could overthink it, Trudy pulled up

Emily's phone number and dialed. It was the first time in years she felt she could rely on someone.

"Trudy, hey!" Trudy could imagine Emily whisking around the kitchen of the Italian restaurant, preparing for a big dinner rush. "What's up?"

Trudy took a long, staggered breath. "I was just wondering," she began, "if you'd heard from your best friend, Allegra, recently?"

Emily was quiet. There was the sound of footsteps and the opening and closing of a door. "I didn't know if I should tell you. I mean, gosh. I hoped I wouldn't have to."

Trudy closed her eyes tightly, and red spots formed in her dark vision. "She's blonde? Skinny? Sort of looks like you, but meaner?" As soon as she said it, Trudy regretted it. But she didn't have the bandwidth to censor herself right now.

"She called me last night to tell me she was in town," Emily explained. "I didn't take the call, but she texted me afterward."

"Is she staying around?"

"I don't know," Emily said. "I haven't figured out if I want to talk to her at all."

"That makes sense."

"Where did you see her?" Emily asked.

"I went out to the Christmas tree farm to surprise Jack," Trudy said. "How stupid am I?"

"Honey! You're not stupid!"

"I feel like an imbecile," Trudy returned as her stomach tied into knots. She considered dropping out of her car and laying on the pavement of the gas station. She wasn't sure how she would find the strength to drive back to Hollow's Grove, let alone get through the festival.

"What are you doing tonight?" Emily asked. "You shouldn't be alone."

"I don't want to be a burden," Trudy said quietly, feeling like the most pathetic woman on earth.

"Don't be silly," Emily said. "I'm finishing up at the restaurant now. I'll bring you Italian food, plenty of wine, and a listening ear. Nina will be there, too."

Trudy didn't bother to drive back to the Hollow's Grove. Feeling frantic, she beelined for Emily's house, where Nina opened the door as she turned into the driveway. The sight of that smile brought a wave of calm over Trudy.

"We're making hot cocoa," Nina said as she swallowed Trudy in a hug. "I hope you like plenty of marshmallows?"

Rex and Nina's two children were in the kitchen eating too many marshmallows, filling their cheeks. Trudy sat next to Nina's little girl as she plopped marshmallows into her hot cocoa and told her a story about her Barbies. Trudy allowed herself to drop into her imagination for a little while, hoping that her stories would destroy the power Jack had over her.

When Emily returned a little while later, Rex took the children upstairs to leave Nina, Emily, and Trudy to the matter at hand. Emily placed to-go boxes filled with her gorgeous Italian food in the center of the table and handed Trudy a fork.

"You'll feel better if you eat something," she instructed.

Trudy twirled spaghetti and Bolognese around and around a fork. Nina dug into the lasagna as Emily spooned herself a bite of gnocchi. As Trudy chewed and swallowed, anxiety loosened out of her shoulders.

"Have you heard from Jack?" Emily asked.

"I haven't looked at my phone," Trudy admitted. "I'm too scared."

"Maybe he has a reason," Nina suggested.

"For going back to Allegra?" Trudy asked, arching her eyebrow.

"She's been gone a long time," Emily reminded them. "Maybe she just came to apologize?"

Trudy's throat was tight, and it was difficult to speak. "You should have seen the way they were looking at each other. It was deathly serious. I realized just how unserious my relationship with Jack is, you know? I'm just his Christmas fling. His distraction, while he waits for Allegra to figure out what she wants."

"You don't know that for sure." But Emily's face echoed enough doubt to confirm Trudy's suspicion. Emily had known Allegra for years; she'd known the density of Allegra and Jack's love. Trudy had been foolish to believe she could mean anything to anyone after such an intense relationship.

"It's totally okay," Trudy continued, twirling another round of spaghetti around her fork. "My original plan was to go back to Boston at the beginning of January, anyway. I'm embarrassed to admit I'd had second thoughts about that."

Nina and Emily exchanged worried glances.

"I'm sorry to hear that," Emily said. "It's been so nice having you here. I've felt almost like Aunt Danika sent you for a reason."

Nina nodded somberly. "It sounds silly, but I've felt the same way. Like our families are supposed to be together." She laughed before adding, "I was even talking to Rex about moving our family back here after I finish medical school. Burks Falls could use another few doctors."

Trudy allowed her shoulders to drop. She couldn't let these kind words distract her from her true purpose. Back in Boston, she had her coffee franchise, a rent-controlled apartment, a grocery store she liked on the corner and the Ramen place down the block. She had Monica, who was sort-of a friend. Maybe she could reach out to the friends she'd abandoned after Ben died. Maybe there was still a life to cling to there.

Emily touched Trudy's elbow. "You have to do what's right for you. We understand that."

"What's going to happen with the inn?" Nina asked.

Trudy sighed. "I don't know. I hate to admit it, but my initial plan was to close down after the holidays and sell the place."

Nina's face darkened. "I suppose that's the practical thing," she offered.

"It sounds horrible," Trudy hurried to say. "Maybe Frankie can take over? She loves that place."

But Trudy knew Frankie was too old to take on such a tremendous task. She would refuse.

"I have to think," Trudy said.

"Let's just get through the festival," Emily said. "After that, you can think hard about what you want to do. And we'll support you, no matter what."

Trudy remembered the float, which she, Frankie, and the other staff members had just completed hours ago.

"I have a request."

"What can we do?" Nina raised her forkful of lasagna.

"We finished the float today," Trudy continued. "It's extraordinary looking, but not because of me. Frankie's a world-class designer." Trudy smiled, remembering how Frankie had thrown herself completely into the work. "I was wondering if the two of you would stand on the float with me during the festival. The plan is to play Christmas music and throw candy."

"Oh! That sounds wonderful!" Emily squeezed Nina's hand. "What's the theme of the float? Do you have a photo?"

"The theme is friendship," Trudy said softly. "You'll see it on Saturday."

"The expectation is killing me!" Emily smiled wide and piled gnocchi on her fork.

"I can't wait," Nina said.

Not long afterward, Trudy's newly adopted family found other topics, ways of distracting Trudy from the cracks in her already broken heart. Sometimes, Trudy even caught herself weighing up the idea of remaining in Wilmington without Jack by her side. As night crawled across the night sky and cast them in shadows, Emily lit several candles on the table and convinced Trudy to stay the night.

"We have a cozy guest bedroom waiting for you," she said. "I can't bear the thought of you driving through the darkness in this cold."

It didn't take too much prodding to convince Trudy to stay. Perhaps due to the stress of the day, fatigue nudged her to bed by ten. She clambered into the guest bedroom and changed into a big t-shirt and a pair of pajama pants. Only then did she convince herself to look at her cell phone.

There was, in fact, a message from Jack.

JACK: Hello! Murphy told me you stopped by the farm today. I'm sorry I missed you.

JACK: I hope everything is all right.

Trudy made up her mind not to text him back. She couldn't shake what she'd seen. It was proof of a past she couldn't overcome, a world between Jack and Allegra that was far more powerful than anything Trudy and Jack could build. That had to be okay. After all, Trudy had already built an entire universe with Ben. She had her memories. That had to be enough.

# Chapter Eighteen

Thankfully, Trudy didn't have much time to think about Jack for the next couple of days. The Festival of Frost Floats was a logistical nightmare, requiring last-minute permits, another food truck request after a drop-out, and the transfer of funds to the community center for the toy drive. Three businesses still hadn't paid their dues, and Trudy spent several hours Friday morning trying to reach someone to ensure that happened on time. "I'm sorry! We got so caught up in decorating the float that we forgot ourselves," a woman at the shoe store said with a laugh. Trudy tried to keep herself upbeat in return. It was a struggle.

But by Friday afternoon, the transfer to the community center was on its way. Trudy breathed a sigh of relief when she received confirmation, along with news that three staff volunteers were heading out today and tomorrow to pile their carts with toys. Word had spread to families in the area that all Christmas toys would be available on Sunday morning, Christmas Eve.

When Trudy had been five or six, she'd received three Christmas presents. Santa had supposedly left them next to the couch, as Trudy's mother hadn't been able to afford a Christmas tree. Trudy remembered unwrapping each of them, her heart bursting with expectation. One had been a plastic horse with a long, plastic mane that looked as though it was blown back in an imaginary wind. Another had been a coloring book with four crayons— blue, yellow, green, and red. The final had been an action figure of the Hulk. Another little girl might have wrinkled her nose at the present, but Trudy had been captivated by it. She'd never had an action figure before, and she treated it the way other little girls treated their dolls. She'd named him Harry and carted him with her everywhere. He'd been a necessary friend in a lonely childhood.

Trudy now realized that her lonely childhood and her lonely adulthood had quite a bit in common, save for the fact that she no longer lived in poverty. For a decade or so in between, she'd had Ben; she'd had love. But that had been an outlier, not the norm.

On the morning of the Festival of Frost Floats, Trudy awoke at five and went for a long walk downtown, engaging in the soft pink light of the sunrise as it rolled over the mountains and blew color along the river. When she returned to the inn, she worked the front desk all morning, ensuring every current guest knew where to go for the festival. She'd even had maps of the parade route printed.

"The floats start here in Wilmington, loop through Burks Falls, and return to Wilmington," she explained to a married couple, incoming guests. "Most of the food trucks and drink stalls will be here in Wilmington, but there are several positioned around Burks Falls, as well.

Burks Falls is an adorable little town, so if you don't make it there during the festival, make sure you go before you leave the area."

"We didn't know about this festival!" The woman beamed and clutched the map. "Jeffrey, isn't it wonderful? We picked the very best weekend to come!"

Most of the current guests of the Hollow's Grove planned to check out on Christmas Eve. They would return to their hometowns, to their families and friends. But Jeffrey and his wife, the married couple at the front desk now, planned to check out on the 27th, two days after Christmas. Trudy wondered why. Perhaps nothing awaited them at home? Maybe they had children who'd decided not to return for the holidays, or there was too much pain in a lackluster Christmas spent at home.

It was true that Christmas could be a heinous time for lonely people. Trudy had spent many years working at The Lucky Bean on Christmas Day, making cappuccinos and lattes for those who whisked in and out, wishing her Merry Christmas on their way to their family parties. Trudy had wanted to ask them to stop saying it. It was a consistent reminder of just how separate she was from the real world.

Max from the Hollow's Grove graciously agreed to connect his truck to the Hollow's Grove float and drive them through the parade route. "I did it last year," he said proudly. "Olivia told me it takes a lot of patience and attention."

Trudy rode up front in Max's truck while Frankie and her husband, Hank, sat on the float itself, holding hands as they creaked toward downtown. As they went, several other trucks hauled Christmas floats to the center of town, where Trudy had assigned everyone a position. The

PNCS Bank was set to start the festival parade with their ice fishing-themed float, followed by the Wilmington Youth Soccer League with their soccer-themed float. The Hollow's Grove was toward the back of the line. If Trudy's calculation was correct, it would wheel past Helen's house at approximately seven-forty-five p.m. It was absolutely essential that Helen see the photograph displayed in all its Christmas glory.

What would Trudy do if Helen wasn't outside? She would cross that bridge when she came to it.

Downtown Wilmington was gorgeous. As though she'd ordered it directly from God himself, snow fluttered from thick gray clouds, and Wilmington locals bustled about with mugs of hot cocoa and boxes of food from the numerous food trucks. After Max parked the truck, putting himself in-line with the other parade attendees, Trudy said, "Meet back here in forty-five?"

"Perfect," Max said. "Gives me enough time to load up on food!"

Trudy whisked around downtown, asking all vendors if they needed anything, checking up on parade floats, and ensuring everything was set. Emily texted that she and Nina were enjoying a glass of hot wine before the parade, and Trudy hurried over to say hello. She felt as though she floated above everything. The spirit of the festival had ignited her.

"We cannot wait to see the float!" Nina exclaimed.

As soon as Nina and Emily returned their mugs, Trudy led them toward their position in the parade. The minute they spotted the photograph, both Emily and Nina stalled on the sidewalk, their eyes glistening.

"Aunt Danika," Emily breathed, touching her chest.

"It's perfect," Nina agreed.

"I wanted to celebrate all they were to one another," Trudy said, her voice wavering. She paused for a moment, not sure if she wanted to open this can of worms. "Ever since I found this photograph, I haven't been able to shake thoughts of Helen. I can't believe what she did to you both. But, as a loner myself, I can't help but think she regrets it, too. That the loneliness has become so thick that she can't see through it."

Nina and Emily studied Trudy ponderously. She had no idea what they were thinking. Would they tell her to stay out of their business?

"The parade will go past Helen's house," Trudy admitted.

"Is that so?" Emily's tone was difficult to decipher.

"I'm sure she hasn't seen this photograph in years," Trudy continued, her voice breaking. "Maybe it'll remind her of something. Maybe she'll come back to herself."

Emily and Nina locked eyes with one another. Trudy imagined them turning on their heels, abandoning her with her silly float. Perhaps they would laugh about her later. They would wonder, sincerely, why that "crazy woman" wanted to ruffle so many feathers.

"I can't imagine she'll feel anything at all," Emily said softly. "But it's a wonderful tribute to what Danika, Olivia, and even my mother were to one another once upon a time."

Nina touched Trudy's elbow. "Thank you, Trudy. Really."

Trudy blinked back tears, still not sure whether to believe them. "Do you still want to ride on the float?"

"We wouldn't miss it," Emily assured her.

"We even bought a few bags of candy to throw," Nina

said, gesturing toward her massive purse. "And eat for ourselves." She winked.

The air shifted. Trudy had the strangest instinct to ask them to forgive her, to apologize profusely. But it seemed that Emily and Nina didn't need that from her.

From somewhere far behind came the sound of Trudy's name. Trudy turned without thinking to find a man in a thick red flannel coat barreling through the crowd. His eyes were manic, and his black hair flew out behind him.

"Is that Jack?" Emily asked.

Trudy's heart blasted against her ribcage. *Not here*, she wanted to tell him. Not now. She had too much to do with the festival; too many people were relying on her to ensure this came together. If she broke down in front of everyone, here on the sidewalk next to the floats, their faith in her would deplete.

But Jack was now only fifteen feet away. He slowed his smile, a mix of hopeful and frightened.

"We'll grab a spot on the float," Emily said, squeezing Trudy's shoulder as they passed. "Good luck."

Trudy couldn't drum up a smile for Jack. He stood before her in all his Paul Bunyan glory, his dark eyebrows stitching together with confusion. Unfortunately, he looked more handsome than ever.

"Trudy! Hey. I've been trying to get a hold of you."

Trudy crossed her arms over her chest and forced herself to remember what Jack and Allegra had looked like together.

"I've been really busy with the festival," Trudy explained. "Is everything okay? Is your float in place?"

"We're in place. Murphy is set to drive the truck, and I promised to stand out on the float and wave in this ridiculous costume." Jack gestured cartoonishly. "I even have a fake balloon ax."

"Thanks for participating," Trudy said.

Jack's smile fell from his face. "Do you think we could talk?" His tone was dark.

"We don't need to talk about anything," Trudy said. "I have a million things to do tonight. Maybe I'll see you around before I head back to Boston?"

Before Jack could stutter with apologies for being unable to love her, Trudy heard her name called from one of the neighboring floats. It seemed they'd parked in the incorrect position, about three blocks away from where they were supposed to go, and Trudy had to direct them around the corner to help them into place. By the time they got there, it was five minutes before the start of the parade. Toward the front, the marching band was warming up, their horns blaring through the night sky. Expectation brimmed on everyone's faces as they opened their hearts and minds for a night of Christmas spectacle.

"How was that?" Emily asked as Trudy clambered onto the float.

"Fine!" Trudy insisted.

"Are you sure?" Emily asked. "He looked like he really wanted to talk to you."

"It's not important," Trudy said, waving her hand. "Frankie? Should we start the speakers?"

"I'm on it!" Frankie reached toward the system Max had helped them install and flicked it on. The first song on the playlist was "Silver Bells," the old Bing Crosby version, and his wonderful, old-fashioned voice sent shivers down Trudy's spine. One night last week, before everything had fallen apart with Jack, they'd slow-danced to this song in the light of the fire at the Hollow's Grove, his big hand cradling hers. She'd felt protected. She'd fallen deeper and deeper in love.

But that was the thing about falling in love. It opened you up to loss. Trudy had lost Ben, and now, she was losing Jack, too. She had to be okay with that. She had to find a way to open herself up again and again.

# Chapter Nineteen

With Max driving slowly and steadily, the Hollow's Grove Inn float cruised down Main Street, beneath strings of glinting Christmas lights, alongside town hall, the riverbed dotted with snowmen, the bowling alley, and the Christmas-decorated windows of local boutiques and bookstores. They passed bouncing children, all bundled up in layers upon layers of sweaters and mittens and scarves, over-sugared with hot cocoa and as much candy as they could get. Emily, Nina, Trudy, Hank, and Frankie threw more candy and clapped or waved along to the next round of songs that came from the speakers— "Frosty the Snowman," "Carol of the Bells," and "Have Yourself a Merry Little Christmas." And for a little while, Trudy allowed herself to forget the frantic look in Jack's eyes as he'd begged her to talk to him.

At seven-thirty, the parade approached the outer edges of downtown Burks Falls. Remarkably, the crowds had hardly dissipated between the two towns, with several festival attendees choosing to sit on the backs of their cars or trucks and watch the floats cruise through the night. Burks Falls offered additional food, wine, and cocoa stalls, and Burks Falls residents milled through downtown, waving excitedly. It was decorated just as immaculately as Wilmington, with no building untouched by Christmas garlands or strings of lights.

Just before the float turned onto Helen's road, Emily turned toward Nina and Trudy. Her face was stricken, and she dropped forward to grip her knees.

"Emily! Are you okay?" Trudy asked.

Emily shook her head. "I don't know if I can do this."

Nina placed her hand on her mother's back and nodded. "When the float stops again, we can just get off."

As Emily nodded in agreement, Trudy's heart surged with fear. This was the final part of her plan. She was so close.

"Emily," Trudy interjected, searching for the right words. "I just don't understand this. Your mother abandoned you when you were pregnant. It's borderline criminal. But still, you do all you can for her from a distance." Trudy puffed out her cheeks. "I know it's just a photograph. What good can a photograph do? But I just can't help but think, when she sees it, she'll have an inkling of just how much she messed up— and how willing you are to mend things."

The parade had stalled. The float hovered on the corner of Helen's street, with the photograph on display for the house immediately to the right of Helen's. Trudy could imagine Helen locked inside with the curtains drawn from Christmas cheer. How could she force her out?

"It's a little more complicated than that," Emily said quietly.

"What do you mean?"

Emily rubbed her eyes so that black makeup smeared around the edges. "On the night Nina was born, my parents decided to forgive me. They were on their way to the hospital when they got into a horrible accident."

Trudy couldn't breathe. Despite the noise of the speaker system and the marching band up ahead, the world dimmed around her.

"They didn't tell me till after Nina was born," Emily continued, her voice breaking. "But my father didn't make it. He died at the hospital, just a few floors away from where I was giving birth. My mother was mostly unscathed, but she refused to see me after that. She wouldn't even speak to me at the funeral."

Trudy was speechless. All those years ago, one night had splintered Helen from her daughter and granddaughter, potentially forever. And she'd allowed her anger and resentment to strengthen, day by day until it was the only thing she could cling onto.

"My mother hates Christmas," Emily continued. "She locks herself away every winter and refuses to celebrate." Emily's chest heaved. "I don't want to make her life worse, Trudy. I really just want to leave her alone. That's what she wants."

Nina held onto her mother and spoke to her quietly, coaxingly. Trudy half-expected them to jump off the float at any second to grab a bus back to Wilmington. Trudy had meddled in their business in a way that was probably hazardous to their mental health. How could she have been so foolish?

The minute she returned to Boston, she told herself, she would keep her head down. She wouldn't bother anyone. She would focus on her coffee shops and continue to build the business. She would be very rich and very alone— like Ebenezer Scrooge.

Emily shifted back up, adjusting her blonde hair behind her ears. She set her jaw. The parade still hadn't moved, which probably meant there was a traffic debacle up ahead. On the other side of the float, Frankie and Hank tossed chocolates at a group of kids, smiling happily, untouched by Emily, Trudy, and Nina's drama. Emily raised her eyes to the photograph, which seemed far too large this close-up. It was almost as though Olivia, Danika, Helen, and Helen's husband were right there with them, standing on the float.

"But you're right, Trudy," Emily breathed. "I have to keep trying. I have to let her know I still love her, no matter what."

With that, Emily grabbed Nina's hand and scrambled from the float. Nina stumbled after her, abandoning the street and disappearing in the soft darkness, away from the shimmering lights of the parade. Trudy held her breath until all she could see were the flashes of light from their fluorescent blonde hair. There was no way to know what would happen next. All she could do was hope for a miracle.

# Chapter Twenty

Helen had never known the Festival of Frost Floats parade to pass by her house. Ordinarily, it was three or four streets away, the sound of the marching band and Christmas music floating at a safe distance. Every other year, Helen pulled her curtains, turned up her television, and abandoned the world.

Yet this year, for reasons that were beyond her, the parade passed directly by her home. She'd first heard the marching band at around six-fifty and scurried to the window to peer out. Incredulously, the first Christmas float appeared, a fishing-themed float created by a local bank. People milled along her sidewalk, some of them even stepping onto her lawn, and rage tightened in her chest. She thought about calling the police and demanding that they get these people off of her property. On a secondary glance, she'd realized there were already about fifteen police officers outside, ensuring nobody got too close to the vehicles. Several of the officers were wearing Santa hats. It was clear they weren't on her side.

Since this horrific discovery, Helen had tightened the

curtains over the windows and turned up her television nearly as loud as it could go. She watched an action film, nothing she cared about, in which Keanu Reeves did a bunch of stunts on screen. Even though it was terribly loud, with gunshot blasts and squealing tires, it did little to block out the Christmas songs outside.

Helen was miserable. She wasn't sure she'd been this miserable in her life. She tried to speak to Brian as a way to calm herself, demanding of him, "Why don't you go out there and tell everyone to leave us alone?" But Brian wasn't there to answer her. The Christmas music seemed only to get louder as time passed.

Just when Helen thought she might have to get in her car and drive her way out of the parade traffic— perhaps all the way to Florida, where warm weather would destroy everyone's cheerful holiday mood— there was a knock at the door. Helen froze. On-screen, Keanu Reeves was sweating like crazy, and his eyes were dark and piercing. She had no idea what was happening in the story. Who on earth would knock on her door right now? Maybe it was Beth, her neighbor. Maybe Beth had made a batch of hot cocoa and wanted to watch the parade together. Maybe if Helen didn't answer it, Beth would get the hint and leave her alone.

But a third and then a fourth knock forced Helen to her feet. If it really was Beth, maybe it was time for Helen to tell her once and for all what she thought of her. As she neared the door, the Christmas music from the parade grew louder and louder. It sounded as though the floats were frozen in place, stuck on her street due to traffic or a marching band incident or a parade float gone awry. The parade would probably never end.

"What is it?" Helen demanded as she yanked open the door with a huff.

But Beth wasn't on her porch with two mugs of cocoa. Rather, two beautiful blonde women held hands and gazed at Helen with fragile, worried eyes. Helen's heart cracked at the edges, even as she heard herself demand, "What are you doing here?" Her voice wavered with confusion, and she didn't sound half as mean as she'd wanted to.

"We wanted to show you something, Mom," Emily said, stepping away from Nina to point toward the street.

Helen followed Emily's finger toward a Christmas float on the corner. An image sat upon the float, something Helen remembered seeing long ago. It almost looked as though it was part of a dream.

The photograph perched on the float was an enormous rendering of Olivia, Danika, Helen, Brian, and baby Emily. In it, the adults were in their twenties, their faces nourished, unwrinkled, and filled with laughter. Baby Emily looked happy as ever, wearing that lace dress Helen remembered sewing herself. She'd been so careful about the detail, wanting her baby to look perfect. Brian was just as handsome as the day she'd married him, just as wonderful as the day he'd passed away. Seeing him like this, on display for all to see, tugged at her heartstrings.

With a jolt, she remembered: Helen and Emily were the only people still alive in that photograph. And Helen had hardly spoken to Emily since Nina's birth. She'd never even met her granddaughter, the gorgeous woman before her. Why? Why had she let so much time pass? Why was she standing in a dark foyer with the curtains closed, her heart blackened against holiday cheer?

"What is this?" Helen finally managed to ask. She

blinked rapidly, trying to get rid of her tears, but she couldn't control them. They fell swiftly and dotted her sweater.

"It's the Hollow's Grove Frost Float. Nina, Trudy, and I have been up there, shivering and waving to everyone all night," Emily explained, her voice breaking. "Seeing your photograph there beside us all night long has broken my heart, Mom. Because I know Danika would want you up there with us. She wouldn't have wanted us to go so long without talking. Please." Emily extended her gloved hand toward Helen. "Won't you join us?"

Helen was speechless. For a long time, she stared down at Emily's hand as memories coursed through her. She thought of that horrific day when the EMT workers had told her Brian wasn't going to make it. Meanwhile, on a separate floor, Emily was in labor with her grandchild—and Helen hadn't had the strength to go see her. She thought of her own labor with Emily, of how Brian had held her hand and told her stories about Burks Falls' legends, about the giants in the Adirondacks and the mermaids in the Falls. Back then, everything had felt possible. Her life had shivered with vitality and hope.

She hadn't believed in anything in a long time. Why, then, should she take her daughter's hand? Why shouldn't she return to her living room and focus on Keanu Reeves' next action scene? It was as good as anything else.

"Mom," Emily said, her voice cracking. "Don't let us go."

Out on the street, the parade had started up again. The floats purred slowly down the road full of sleigh bells that adorned each side, and children chased after them, hungry for more candy. The photograph of Danika, Olivia, Helen, Brian, and Emily grew closer and closer until it looked like Danika stared directly into Helen's home.

A few years after Nina's birth, Danika had come to Helen's home, stood out here on this porch, and slammed her fist against the door until Helen had answered. "You need to meet your granddaughter," she'd insisted. "You need to know her and love her the way I know her and love her. You're her grandmother." But Helen had told Danika to go away. She'd told her she'd betrayed her.

And when she'd learned of Danika's spontaneous death? Helen had curled in a ball in bed and hoped that death would come for her, too. There was no reason she was still alive, not when so many of her family members had gone.

Yet, here was Emily, and here was Nina. And they wanted her to come with them.

"Let's get your coat, Grandma," Nina said sweetly. Helen remembered having heard through the grapevine that Nina was in medical school. Brian would have been so proud of her.

Helen nodded and stepped back to find her shoes. Her arms and legs shook violently as she put herself together, drawing a hat tightly over her ears and zipping her coat to her chin.

"Let's go! Let's go!" Emily said, her smile enormous. Helen remembered Emily as a little girl, begging for Helen and Brian to come out to play in the snow. Finally, she drew her gloved hand over Emily's and allowed herself to be led. Nina closed the door behind them, and Helen didn't even think about locking it. Who would steal from her tonight during the Festival of Frost Floats? Burks

Falls was a quiet and loving community. It's why she and Brian had decided to stay here to raise Emily.

The woman who greeted them on the Hollow's Grove Frost Float looked a bit like Olivia. Helen could see her in her dark curls and her brown eyes and in the way she tilted her head as she said hello, as though she was frightened of saying the wrong thing.

"My name is Trudy," she said as she helped Helen onto the float.

"I'm Helen." Helen blinked up at the enormous photograph. Had it been taken on that day when they'd decorated the very first Hollow's Grove Frost Float? She couldn't be sure. But there was a magic in their eyes that suggested it.

Tentatively, Helen reached out to touch the photograph, which had been printed on a large canvas. She touched her sister's hand and her husband's face. She touched baby Emily's cheek as her eyes spilled tears.

The speaker system on the float played "The Christmas Song," a song that ached with nostalgia. All Helen had ever wanted was to have a family and grow old with Brian. All she'd wanted was blissful Christmas dinners and blankets of snow outside. She and Brian had adored the Festival of Frost Floats and had complimented Danika endlessly, telling her that her work was essential in the community. That they wanted to help her every year afterward.

"Isn't it magical, Mom?" Emily whispered into her ear, steadying her with a hand at her lower back.

Helen pulled her eyes away from the photograph to gaze out at the crowds. They crept along her street and turned the corner to head downtown. Nina kept glancing back at her mother and grandmother with tears in her eyes as Trudy tossed candy to children and adults alike. Two other people were on the float, a man and a woman with similar bottle-neck glasses.

Before Helen knew what she was doing, she raised her hand and waved toward the crowd. Several children waved back, their eyes alight as they took in the float, the magical lights, and the heaps of fake snow. The sharp wind on her cheeks didn't feel half as sharp as it normally did, as though she was protected by something. She touched her cheeks and realized she was still smiling. It felt unnatural.

The parade finished in Wilmington, the neighboring town where Danika, Emily, and Nina had lived together — only fifteen minutes from Helen, yet so far in many ways. As the parade petered out, Trudy leaped from the float, hurrying off somewhere.

"It's her first year planning it," Emily explained. "There was a whole lot more to it than I remembered. Danika and Olivia never let on everything they were doing."

Helen gazed out across downtown Wilmington, where people milled between food trucks, drink stalls, and carnival games. If she wasn't totally mistaken, she was pretty sure she recognized a few faces in the crowd— people she hadn't seen since before she'd sequestered herself inside. Was that Brian's friend from work? Was that one of the girls from the country club? Gosh, it was bizarre to be back in the world again.

"Do you want to get something to eat, Mom?" Emily asked.

"I've heard amazing things about the chicken place," Nina said, pointing to a food truck far down the road.

"I know what I want to eat," Helen said, her eyes widening.

"Anything!" Emily assured her.

Helen swallowed. "I want to go to your restaurant, Emily." Saying it aloud minimized just how much it meant to her. All she'd wanted in the world for years was to taste Emily's gorgeous Italian food. She wanted to know the full breadth of her daughter's talents.

"Then we shall go to my restaurant!" Emily smiled and dropped down from the float, where she raised her hand to help Helen to the street. "It's too crowded here, anyway."

Helen swallowed the lump in her throat and followed behind Emily through the thrumming crowd. On a stage near the town hall, Olivia's niece introduced the next band, all of whom held guitars or drumsticks and wore Santa hats. She waved to Emily, Helen, and Nina as they passed by and gave a thumbs-up. Helen wasn't sure what that meant. She felt on the brink of tears at all times.

Helen recognized Emily's car from her recent trip from the hospital. Nina instructed her to sit in the passenger seat while she dropped into the back and buckled her seat belt. Snow flickered across the front window, melting as the heat intensified.

"It was cold out there," Emily breathed. There was a hint of optimism in her voice, as though she'd dreamed of a night like this for years. Helen hoped she wouldn't disappoint her daughter. She hoped Emily hadn't dreamed up a different version of Helen, one that didn't exist.

Emily's restaurant was in full swing. Apparently, after the Festival of Frost Floats petered out in Burks Falls, plenty of folks had wandered down to the Italian restaurant for a late dinner. Families were stuffed around tables, with extra chairs retrieved from the attic. Emily laughed as she entered and waved at the hostess familiarly.

"Rough night?"

"We thought we would close early!" The hostess shook her head. "And then suddenly, it was like a stampede."

"Emily, you know, we don't have to do this right now," Helen said, feeling foolish. "It's way too busy. I don't want to overwhelm you."

Emily turned and locked her eyes with Helen's. "I'll set up a table in my office." She then reached behind the hostess stand to grab two menus and pass them to Helen and Nina. "Order whatever you like. I made almost all of the sauces this morning, and the recipes are all mine." She said it proudly, wanting Helen to know how far she'd pushed her career.

Helen opted for lasagna, while Nina went with tortellini. Emily led them through the chaos of the front restaurant, through a back hallway, and into her office. Given what Helen remembered of Emily's chaotic teenage bedroom, Helen was surprised at the neatness of the office, at the clean desk and the photographs that hung on the wall in a straight line. One of them was of Emily, Nina, and Danika when Nina had been a baby— a time when Helen's grief had been insurmountable. When Nina ran to the bathroom, and Emily went to the kitchen to order their food, Helen stared at the photograph for a long time. She'd robbed herself of so much time.

Emily returned with three glasses of wine, and Nina came a second later. Both of them smiled at Helen with a mix of curiosity and fear, as though she were a wild animal they weren't sure they could trust yet. After Emily set up a portable table, they sat around it, all at a loss for words.

Helen remembered Brian's eyes on the last night he'd been alive— when he'd learned of Emily going into labor with Nina. He'd known their daughter needed them. He'd longed to be by her side, no matter what.

*I made it, Brian,* Helen thought.

Helen raised her glass and said, "Merry Christmas. I'm sorry it took me so long." Her voice was tentative and strange. She'd never been so open with her feelings. It was a start.

One of the kitchen staff members brought their food soon after and placed the heaping platters on the table, along with a small bowl of freshly grated parmesan. Helen couldn't remember the last time she'd had Italian food, and her mouth watered.

Emily watched her expectantly, nervously, as Helen placed the tongs of her fork in the melted cheese on top of the lasagna. Helen had never considered the fact that Emily wanted Helen to try her food just as much as Helen yearned to taste it.

"I'm so nervous," Emily said with a soft laugh.

Helen lifted the bite of lasagna to her lips, bringing with it several long strings of cheese. She closed her eyes as she placed the bite on her tongue and closed her lips, caught in a spectacular moment of cheese, sauce, meat, and garlic. It was a firework of flavor. As she chewed and swallowed, she allowed her eyes to open once more, and she peered at her daughter, incredulous.

"So?" Emily sounded petrified. "What did you think?"

Helen's shoulders dropped. What was the appropriate language for something like this? How could she explain to her daughter just how much this meant?

"It's perfect, Emily," Helen said, her eyes filling with tears again. "It's the best thing I've ever tasted. I could eat this the rest of my life and never get sick of it."

Emily laughed and burst to her feet to hug Helen again. Nina urged Helen to try the tortellini and begged Emily to go back to the kitchen to get a helping of gnocchi, too. "She has to try that next!"

Somehow, the curse was broken. Helen fell into her daughter and granddaughter's voices easily, enraptured with their laughter. She heard herself asking questions about Nina's medical school and field of study. Emily asked Helen's opinion about what to cook for Christmas, which was just two days away. "But you're coming, aren't you?" Emily asked, her eyes widening.

How could Helen say no? Now that she was back in the world, she wanted to feel, taste, hear, and experience all of it. She didn't want to say no to things anymore.

## Chapter Twenty-One

Trudy couldn't believe it was nearly over. She stood in the festival crowd alongside Frankie, Hank, and Max, watching a local band perform a jazzy version of "Jingle Bell Rock," swaying with a mug of hot wine in her hands. It was nearly eleven o'clock at night, far past most everyone's bedtime in the cozy and sleepy town of Wilmington. However, the food stalls were still open; people still purchased hot cocoa and hot wine. A part of Trudy wondered if they would keep this up all night and into Christmas Eve morning. A part of her hoped they would. The minute she returned to the inn and got into bed alone, the weight of the previous few days was sure to crash in on her and drive her up the wall.

As the song faded out, Frankie turned and shook her head. "I wish Olivia could have seen this festival. It was much bigger than anything she put on!"

This surprised Trudy. "Really?"

Frankie nodded. "Ordinarily, Olivia had about half

the number of food and wine stalls and less than half the number of Frost Floats!"

Nobody had told this to Trudy, not in all her weeks of planning. "That's a surprise!"

"It's not," Frankie insisted. "Everyone is finally recognizing all the tremendous work and goodwill Olivia brought to these communities. They want to pass along that love to you." She touched Trudy's arm delicately, her eyelids heavy with fatigue. She then bent her head and added quietly, "I can't believe Helen got on the float!"

Trudy remained incredulous about that. From the Hollow's Grove float, she'd watched Nina and Emily on Helen's front porch, talking to a woman who looked both forlorn and irate at once. It was horrible what loneliness could do to you. Just when Trudy had decided to give up on Helen, however, she'd slipped into her coat, hat, and gloves and followed after Nina and Emily, clambering onto the float. The way she'd stared at that photograph had made Trudy shiver. Love echoed from her eyes, proof that she remembered the day the photograph had been taken, that she would have done anything to return to that day.

As eleven drifted toward eleven-thirty, a few food trucks closed their doors. The band officially finished their set and wished everyone a Merry Christmas, their smiles exhausted but enormous. Trudy hurried around downtown, where she was inevitably asked a million and a half questions. It seemed nobody had read the instructional email about where to leave the floats or how to recycle their spare materials. The guy who owned the shoe store wanted a list of every single toy the community center had purchased so far, which Trudy explained was impossible. They didn't have time.

When the clock struck midnight, downtown was more-or-less clear. Several people had driven their floats back to where they'd rented them from, ready to get them off of the street in front of their businesses. The food trucks were gone, leaving only trace scents of refried beans and baked dough. Perhaps out of habit, Trudy allowed herself to look for Jack, hunting for the sharp color of his bright red flannel. She didn't see him. Perhaps he was off somewhere with Allegra, cozy beneath a blanket in front of the television. Or maybe they were already fast asleep, preparing for a full day of activity together tomorrow.

As Trudy directed herself back toward the Hollow's Grove, she heard her name and froze. For a moment, she allowed herself to pretend that voice belonged to Jack. But when she turned around, she found Mike, the owner of one of the local banks, hurrying toward her, waving his hand.

"Mike! Hey!" Trudy prepared herself to explain for the umpteenth time where the floats needed to be returned. "Is everything okay?"

Mike gasped for breath and tapped his chest. "I'm sorry to bother you like this. I know you want to get home." His eyes glinted from the Christmas lights strung overhead. "I just wanted to congratulate you on a wonderful festival. I can't remember the town having a better time."

Trudy was touched. "Thank you, Mike. I appreciate that."

Mike dug into the pocket inside his coat, his brows furrowed. A second later, he produced a thick envelope and pressed it into Trudy's hands.

"What is this?" Trudy blinked down at the envelope, upon which someone had scrawled "XMAS."

"My wife and I were talking about it," Mike explained nervously. "We always spoiled our children, but we don't have grandchildren yet. We can't bear the thought of those children not getting all the things they need. And to us, Christmas is about spoiling little ones."

Trudy could hardly believe this. Mike wasn't anyone she knew well— just another owner of a bank in a town too small for anything more than a couple of credit unions. But here, she threw her arms around him and thanked him. He couldn't have known that he'd been the cherry on top of a very complicated day.

The following morning, Trudy awoke at six and drove out to the nearest box store. Bleary-eyed but set on spending the thousand dollars Mike had given her, she hurried through the automatic doors and into the anonymous space, where everything flashed red with a Christmas sale. Not many people were at the box store this early, and an older man in a blue vest waved at her as she scurried past. "Good morning!"

Trudy found herself in the middle of the toy aisle with Mike's envelope burning in her pocket. For a moment, she imagined herself to be the eight-year-old girl from poverty, and she began to fill her grocery cart with everything she could have imagined herself playing with: dolls with big, doe eyes and long lashes; Barbies with fancy dresses and incredible careers; playhouses with slides that took your dolls from the third floor all the way to the pool down below.

After most of her cart was filled with pastels, she moved on to the boys' section and filled a separate cart with toy cars, toy trucks, and action figures— thinking that she would have loved this stuff just as much as a little girl. It would have activated her imagination and taken her out of the sorrowful shadows of the home she'd shared with her mother.

What would her mother say if she could see Trudy now? Trudy stopped to consider this as she hovered over the plastic pandas and black bears and lions, enough figurines to fill the entire animal kingdom. Would Trudy's mother have been proud of her? Would she even have recognized her at all?

Although Trudy had come to terms with her and Ben's inability to have children, she had ached for one, if only to stop the cycle her mother had created. She'd wanted to give her daughter or son a beautiful and love-filled childhood. But it hadn't happened for her and Ben. She'd had to find a way to forgive herself, her body, and Ben's body.

Well, maybe she would never forgive Ben's body for giving up on him like that. A part of her would always ache for the years they would never get to spend together.

Throughout that early morning at the box store, Trudy faded in and out of her own memories and filled three different carts. After a little while, one of the employees approached to ask if she needed help, and she explained she needed to know how much more money she could spend. He set to work, scanning Barbies, plastic animals, and toy trains. She watched him work as the number rose and rose.

"You're almost to one thousand," he explained. "Just sixty-two more dollars."

Trudy was careful about her final selections. She

decided on several dolls, a Monster Truck, some teddy bears, and several boxes of Play-Doh. After the employee scanned everything, he announced she was seven dollars over. That was all right with her.

But when it was over, Trudy blinked down to see she'd filled five carts of toys. It was far more than could fit in her little car and trunk. How would she get it to the community center?

It was nearly eight in the morning, which meant Trudy was needed back at the inn shortly. Her adrenaline around buying Christmas presents had completely robbed her of foresight. She glanced nervously at the box store employees, who smiled openly back at her. They knew the toys were for charity, and they basked in her glow.

It occurred to Trudy, then, that the only person she knew in the world with a big enough vehicle to transport the toys to the community center was Jack Carter. Perhaps she could call him, explain she was happy just being friends, and ask for his help. Allegra could come by, too. They could meet one another officially. If Trudy had even the slightest desire to stay in Wilmington, to build a family with Emily, Helen, and Nina and reconnect with her roots, she needed to face the truth of Jack and Allegra's relationship. She would run into them all the time. That was small-town living for you.

Trudy's phone buzzed. She dared herself to think it was Jack, which only added insult to injury.

"Emily! Hey!" Trudy's voice was overly bright in the box store. "How did it go last night?"

"I can't begin to thank you," Emily said, her voice breaking. "I haven't spent that much time with my mother since 1996."

Trudy's heart lifted as Emily told her what had happened after the festival: that she and Nina had brought Helen to Emily's restaurant, that Helen had opened up gradually, telling stories about Emily's father that Emily had never heard before.

"She even stayed the night!" Emily went on. "She's upstairs right now as I speak! I can't believe it. I'm going to make pancakes and eggs and bacon and toast. I'm going to cook everything in the kitchen. And best of all, my mother will get to meet her great-grandchildren this morning! As soon as she wakes up!"

Emily's voice was filled with ecstasy. It made Trudy feel like she was floating.

"And the parade was sensational all the way through, Trudy," Emily went on. "Everyone is raving about it. There are more than a thousand photographs on social media. A news website wrote an article about our 'spectacular toy drive.' The writer even references Aunt Danika and your Aunt Olivia!"

Trudy smiled down at the massive haul of toys. She felt like a completely different person than she'd been a month ago. How had it happened so quickly?

"I'm just so glad everything came together," Trudy breathed.

"That's not all." Emily sounded hesitant. "But I don't know how to tell you this."

"What are you talking about?" Trudy's anxiety spiked.

"I got a call from Allegra very early this morning," Emily explained. "Probably around two? I was still awake because I couldn't sleep after all those conversations with my mother. My thoughts were too fast."

Trudy couldn't breathe. Her tongue tasted like sand.

"I don't know why I answered it," Emily went on. "Maybe I was curious? My heart was open from talking to Mom. When I answered it, Allegra was crying, but she sounded resolute. She apologized to me for abandoning me. She said for months, she was shrouded in doubt about everything in her life, including her future with Jack, and she just had to get out."

Trudy couldn't imagine anyone in the world wanting to get away from Jack. Was that woman insane?

"She came back to Wilmington this week to try to get him back," Emily explained. "But Jack said no."

Trudy stood in stunned silence. Overhead, the speaker system at the box store projected a voice, telling everyone there was a spill in aisle seven. What time was it? Why was she still at the box store?

"Did you hear me, Trudy?" Emily asked.

"I think so." Trudy shook her head. "I just don't really understand."

"Jack told Allegra he'd met someone else," Emily pushed it. "That she was too late."

Trudy's heart hammered in her chest. None of this was making sense. She'd seen Jack alongside beautiful Allegra at the Christmas tree farm. She'd understood the depths of their love for one another. She'd also remembered the single greatest fact of her life: that she wasn't worthy of love. Her mother had abandoned her, which was the biggest proof of all.

But then again, Trudy remembered Ben had loved her. And Ben was one of the greatest people Trudy had ever met in her life. Maybe that meant something. Maybe that meant she had something in her, something remarkable. It was difficult to say, even at forty-six years old.

"Go see him," Emily instructed. "Do it as soon as you can, Trudy. He's waiting for you."

"I don't know what to say," Trudy breathed.

"Just speak from the heart," Emily told her. "It's all you can do."

After Emily and Trudy got off the phone, Trudy blinked up at one of the box store staff members, the same guy who'd used his price gun to tell her how many more toys she could pick out.

"I can't transport all of these toys right now," she explained. "I need to get a bigger vehicle."

The man frowned, surprised she hadn't thought this through. But Trudy was done thinking properly.

"Can we put them in the back?" Trudy asked. "I'll be here sometime in the next few hours."

"Okay," the man agreed, taking the handle of the first cart. "I'll put them somewhere safe. We're like the North Pole around here." He winked happily, caught up in the spirit of Christmas. But as Trudy bucked out of the box store and into the crisp cold, fear took over, and she wasn't sure she would make it through the next part of her journey. Ultimately, Jack had approached her last night, presumably to tell her what had been going on. And she'd rebuked him. How could she explain just how broken she was? How could she make him understand how much she wanted to heal, if only so they could try again?

# Chapter Twenty-Two

Helen awoke in a strange place. For as long as she could remember, decades upon decades, she'd slept in the bedroom she'd once shared with Brian, where she'd drawn the sheets tightly over the windows to block out the sun. But here, wherever she was, sunlight splintered across the bedspread, and birds twittered outside, outnumbering the ones on her street. She lurched upward and pressed herself against soft pillows, blinking around a beautiful bedroom with white curtains and paintings of lighthouses. Her head throbbed gently as though she'd had something to drink last night. But that wasn't possible. She didn't drink. She never stayed out late, either.

In a rush, everything came back to her. The parade. The photograph of Danika and Olivia. Emily and Nina, her gorgeous daughter and granddaughter. And then—the restaurant, where she, Emily, and Nina had unraveled the events of the previous decades, coming together as a family. Numerous times, Helen had thought maybe she was dreaming it. How was it possible Emily could forgive her so readily?

Now, Helen tip-toed toward the door and peered out at the upstairs hallway. From downstairs came the sound of children squealing, along with the sizzle of something cooking in the kitchen. Helen took a soft step into the hallway, hoping not to be caught. A moment later, a man appeared, wearing a pair of basketball shorts and a big T-shirt. He was in his late forties, maybe, and quite handsome, with salt and pepper hair and strong shoulders. Helen had hardly spoken to any men in the previous years besides her doctor, and the sight of this one caught her off-guard.

"Helen," the man said kindly. "I've been waiting a long time to meet you. I'm Kurt, Emily's husband." He reached out his hand to shake Helen's.

Helen stared at Emily's husband, slightly awestruck. It felt almost like meeting a celebrity.

"I'm so pleased to meet you," Helen said. "I know you've made my daughter very happy."

"Not as happy as she's made me," Kurt said.

Helen remembered how desperately she'd wanted Emily to marry Nina's father, Everett Proctor, a boy she'd never even loved. In fact, Helen had begged Emily to do it, if only to uphold their family legacy and propriety. But so many years later, it didn't matter at all.

Helen had heard that Everett Proctor had turned into a dud, anyway. He'd married his high school sweetheart and almost immediately cheated on her, then kept up that same pattern with his next three wives. Helen was so glad Emily had avoided that heartache. It was as though her instincts had told her to stay away.

Helen and Kurt padded downstairs together to find

Nina, Emily, and Nina's two children bathed in the sunlight that streamed in through the kitchen windows. The children gazed at Helen curiously. Probably, they saw her as a decrepit old woman— her back crooked and her wrinkles etched around her eyes.

"Good morning, Mom!" Emily was happier than Helen had ever seen her. "Alexa? Dean? This is your great-grandmother!"

Alexa and Dean popped up from the chairs around the kitchen table and smiled up at Helen. Just like Nina and Emily, they were tow-headed children. If Helen wasn't mistaken, she thought Dean looked a bit like Brian. She imagined Brian and Dean together somewhere, perhaps fishing along the riverbed. She imagined Brian adjusting Dean's hands around the fishing rod and helping him cast it far over the rushing water.

Nina pressed a cup of coffee into Helen's hands as Helen searched her mind for something to say. She hadn't been around little kids since Emily was small.

"Why don't you show Great-Grandma your drawings?" Nina suggested helpfully.

This was something Alexa and Dean understood. Alexa grabbed her coloring book and flung it forward to show off a picture of all of Santa's reindeer, with Rudolph out front, wearing a tremendously red nose. Alexa, who was maybe two or three, had scribbled through everything. Helen laughed, saying, "Alexa, you really are so talented!"

"Me too!" Dean added his coloring book to the mix. "It's the elves in their workshop."

"Wow. That is really something." Helen set down the coffee and took both papers in her hands, pretending to really analyze them. She felt Alexa and

Dean's pride balloon. Was it always so easy with children?

"I hope you're hungry," Emily said as she breezed past. "I have pancakes and bacon and eggs."

"My goodness, Emily," Helen said with a laugh. "You've fed me non-stop since we met yesterday."

"That's what it's like around here," Kurt explained. "Ever since I met Emily, it's been non-stop delicious food."

"We're spoiled," Nina agreed, touching her husband's shoulder.

For a moment, Nina and Emily gazed at Helen as though neither of them could believe she was there in the kitchen with them. Helen returned the drawings to the great-grandchildren and watched the bacon spit in the skillet, casting its oil across the countertop. It was messy and wild and free in a way her kitchen never was. She had the sudden instinct never to return home— to only stay here with her darling girl and mend her broken heart. Would Emily let her?

It was as though Emily had read her mind.

"I was thinking," Emily said, turning back toward the skillet. "Maybe we could stop by your house later to pick up a few things? Clothes and toiletries and anything else you might like. It's the holidays, and I see no reason you shouldn't be here with all of us."

Helen's throat nearly closed. She took a staggered, tear-filled breath. She hadn't done anything to deserve their kindness.

"What do you think?" Emily asked, turning slightly to gaze at her. "Would you like to stay here for a little while?"

Helen dropped her chin into a nod. "I would love it, Emy."

Emy was what Brian had called her as a little girl when she'd been a little bit like Alexa, small and happy with a bright, flashing ponytail. Emily's eyes glinted with the memory.

"Then it's settled," Emily said, setting her jaw. "Just sit down, Mom. We'll take care of everything."

Helen dropped into one of the kitchen chairs and filled her mouth with nutty coffee, which tasted far better than the drip coffee she normally made at home. It was as though this whole world of emotion, taste, color, and light had always waited here for her. She was finally ready to live in it.

## Chapter Twenty Three

Before Trudy could drive out to the Christmas tree farm, she found herself at the front desk of the Hollow's Grove Inn, up to her ears in late-morning check-outs. Most guests were headed back to their families and friends, back to where they were needed for early-morning Christmas present unwrapping and eggnog-drinking. They were in a hurry, frequently tossing their keys on the counter and waving goodbye as they grabbed their suitcases and fled. Everyone wanted to make good time.

By ten-thirty, everyone set to check out was on their way to wherever it was they'd come from. Around her, the inn creaked softly in the winter winds, the wood of its exterior walls straining. Trudy was stunned at the rush of emotion she felt now, listening to such an empty house. Abstractly, she checked the scheduling book on the front counter, which showed that they were fully booked through January, February, and most of March. If she decided to close the inn, she would need to call all of these people herself and explain. Could she really bring herself to do that?

Trudy stepped into the back dining room to find Max playing solitaire with a deck of cards rather than his phone, like most kids his age. It warmed her heart to see it.

"Max? There's only one couple left in the entire inn," she explained as she laced her arms through her coat. "I'm heading out for a few hours. Give them anything they want and call me if you need anything. When I get back, you can head out early, okay?"

Max thanked her profusely. Apparently, he was playing the organ at church tonight, and he needed a few extra hours to practice. It had never occurred to Trudy that Max could play the organ. She smiled sadly to herself, making a mental note to ask him to play the piano in the main room soon. But did that mean she wanted to stick around long enough for that to happen? Did that mean she wanted to keep the inn alive?

Trudy could barely breathe on her drive to the Christmas tree farm. This was maybe the twentieth time she'd taken this route, but it felt different this time. She had no idea what awaited her on the other end.

When she pulled into the long driveway of the Christmas tree farm, she had to laugh. Obviously, the farm was closed. It was Christmas Eve, after all, and everyone across Wilmington and Burks Falls already had their Christmas trees. The festival had already taken place, with many floats already dismantled. The Christmas trees at the farm were spared another year.

Trudy sat in the driver's seat of her car for a little while, watching snow flutter down across the tips of trees and along the roof of the shack. She half-expected Jack to step out from behind the line of trees and raise a gloved hand to wave.

She remembered the first time she'd seen Jack, just a little more than three weeks ago. She'd been overwrought with emotion, on the verge of tears at any moment. When he'd wanted to unload twenty-five Christmas trees and go on his merry way, she'd wanted to scream. What had she known about operating an inn? At that time, she hadn't even remembered the existence of the Festival of Frost Floats.

The way he'd asked to help her would stick with her forever. He'd seen her drowning, and he'd reached out his hand. It had been a long time since anyone had opened their eyes to see just how far away from the rest of the world she was.

Trudy had only been to Jack's real house a handful of times. It was located around the corner from the Christmas tree farm, hidden by a small forest that seemed to have more than its fair share of gray squirrels. As Trudy drove up the long driveway, she gripped the steering wheel with such intensity that her knuckles turned white. When the driveway curved, she spotted Jack's truck parked next to the wooden cabin, along with a warm glow coming from his front window, proof he had a fire burning in the fireplace.

The front door burst open a split second after Trudy cut the engine. Jack stood in a thick flannel, his beard scraggly and his eyes wet. Trudy got out of her car and stood in the crisp cold, staring up at him. They were like two wild animals in the woods, coming across one another and trying to decide what to do next. She imagined herself like a frightened rabbit and him like a great, big moose.

Brave enough to make the first move, Jack stepped out of the house and stood on the front porch. Trudy stepped away from her car and clipped her door shut. Her breath came in bursts of fog from her mouth.

*Do something*, Trudy told herself. *Don't let this die. Not now. Not when you've come so far*.

"I came to say I'm sorry," Trudy said.

Jack stepped down the porch staircase and crunched in the snow. Even from here, Trudy could smell his musk— a mix of leather and bonfire. She wanted to press her face into his chest and listen to his heartbeat. She wanted the rest of the world to go on without them.

Trudy walked toward him, drawn to him as though he were a magnet. "I came to the farm the other day when you were talking to your ex," she said softly. "I added it to my list of 'reasons never to get close to anyone' and decided to push you away."

"I wish you would have told me," Jack said.

"A healthier person would have told you," Trudy said. "But I'm just in the process of getting healthy. I have a long way to go."

Jack cleared the distance between them so that they were only a foot or so apart. If Trudy reached out, she could draw her fingers through his.

"Allegra showing up like that surprised me," Jack explained softly. "When she left last year, she gave me no explanation. I was reeling for over a year, wondering if everything I'd understood about the world was wrong. Wondering if I could ever patch myself up again."

Trudy nodded. She understood what it felt like when the universe pulled the rug out from under you.

"The past few weeks with you have proven something

to me," Jack went on. "You reminded me of the beauty of the world."

"Me?" It was beyond Trudy's comprehension of herself. Wasn't she too broken to bring such joy to anyone's life?

Jack stepped closer and placed his hands along the curve of her back. Trudy shivered at his touch yet hungered for more of it. With his lips so close to hers, she ached to clear the distance between them.

"I know we're still strangers to one another," Jack said. "In many ways."

Trudy nodded, even though she felt that Jack and Emily already knew her better than anyone back in Boston did.

"But I want to get to know you better," Jack breathed. "I want you in my life. If you'll have me."

Overwhelmed with desire, Trudy rose up on her tiptoes and pressed her lips against Jack's. This was her answer. In opening up her soul to him, she felt the darkness of the past draw itself from her heart and shimmer away, dissolving into the soft, wintry clouds above. When their kiss broke, neither Jack nor Trudy could stop smiling. Birds twittered in the distance, their song echoing through the trees. And when they kissed again, Trudy wasn't sure she would find the will to stop.

But soon afterward, she remembered one of the reasons she'd come.

"I need your truck!" Trudy laughed at how ridiculous it sounded.

Jack's lips glistened from kissing too much. "So that's it. You're using me for my vehicle?"

"Exactly."

Jack laughed. "I should have known it was too good to be true."

"Everything in life is an exchange of goods and services," Trudy joked.

"All right. I'll have to take your word for it." Jack tugged her against him, his hands still on her lower back.

"It's just a short drive," Trudy urged. "We'll be back here in no time."

Back in the passenger seat of Jack's truck, Trudy buckled herself in and watched Jack's sturdy hand as he cut the gearshift up and over into drive. A long time ago, she'd watched her mother drive shift as the thick, fake jewels of her bracelets had jangled. Trudy hoped wherever her mother was, she was all right. She hoped the sun shone on her face and that she had enough food to eat. She hoped she remembered the love little Trudy had wanted to give to her in some small way.

Jack parked out front at the box store. "I never imagined you'd take me here."

"Come on," Trudy ordered, clambering out and guiding him inside, where the same store clerk from earlier helped them wheel all five carts out to the truck. Jack was impressed, especially with the plastic dinosaurs she'd purchased.

"I had so many of these as a kid," he explained as he placed them delicately in the back of his truck.

After the pick-up, they drove over to the community center. Already, the parking lot was stuffed to the gills with parents picking up last-minute Christmas gifts for their children. Trudy and Jack entered with their arms full, heading toward the back table, where the toys were sorted. The community center organizers greeted Trudy as though she were royalty, wrapping her in hugs and thanking her for all her work.

"This is a donation from Mike at the bank," Trudy explained as she placed several dolls tenderly on the table. "And there's a lot more where that came from."

Trudy and Jack stayed at the community center throughout the afternoon, helping them sort and pass out toys and chatting with parents about their Christmas plans. Frequently, they passed one another and squeezed each other's hands, feeling a part of a team.

Not long before the community center closed for the evening, Helen, Emily, and Nina appeared with a final box of toys. The sight of the three generations of Mitchells together warmed Trudy's heart.

"We decided to go on a shopping spree," Emily explained as she rifled through the box, removing a jump rope, several Barbies, and complicated Lego boxes. "Mom has many opinions about the new Barbie dolls."

Helen's cheeks were pink from laughter. "There are so many different kinds! How does any little girl choose which one they want?" She adjusted her sweater over her shoulders and added, "Their costumes are exquisite these days, though."

"I remember you used to sew clothes for my Barbies," Emily said. "Anything I wanted; I could order from you."

Helen's eyes glinted. "I can't believe you remember that."

After their toys were sorted and handed out to parents whipping in and out for last-minute presents, Emily leaned over the table and whispered, "I take it everything went okay today?" She wagged her eyebrows in the direction of Jack, who spoke with another parent, a father wearing a Giants' baseball hat.

"Better than okay," Trudy admitted. "I hate that I jumped to conclusions about that."

Emily raised her shoulders. "You're human. You're probably going to make a lot more mistakes after this one."

"You think?" Trudy laughed. "Gosh. I hoped my days of mistakes were over."

"Buckle up, baby. We're only in our forties," Emily joked. "There's a lot more living to be done."

Trudy's heart lifted. Spontaneously, she reached across the table and hugged Emily close, drawing in a breath of her vanilla perfume. Already, she'd caught herself thinking of Emily as her little sister— a woman with whom she'd shared her innermost secrets. Their relationship had felt almost instantaneous, as though Danika and Olivia had already laid the foundation.

"You'll come to our place for Christmas tomorrow?" Emily asked as their hug broke. "I can't imagine it without you."

Trudy nodded. "I don't know where else I'd rather be."

# Chapter Twenty-Four

The fire in Jack's fireplace crackled and spat, its orange flecks tracing the stones. Trudy wore Jack's flannel shirt and sat, cozied up, on his couch, listening to the Christmas music that purred from the speakers. Jack poured her a mug of cocoa and passed it over, his eyes soft and contented. It was only twenty minutes till Christmas, and Trudy felt completely unlike herself. Perhaps this was the version she'd been meant to be all along.

"Can I be honest about something?" Jack asked as he settled in beside her, bringing with him the smell of pine trees and snow.

"Anything."

Jack swallowed a gulp of hot cocoa. "I'm terrified you're going to go back to Boston and remember how much you love it." He shook his head. "You're a business-woman. You have an entire life there. Maybe this Christmas was just a blip in your story."

Trudy set her mug of cocoa on the coffee table and

took his free hand in hers. "Do you know what I think about when it comes to Boston?"

Jack shook his head.

"I think about the microwaveable dinners I ate almost every night. I think about the pair of slippers I wore almost every day with the hole in the toe. I think about how my best friend was the manager of one of my coffee shops, but that I've never even been to her house." Trudy stuttered as she listed these things out, terrified that she was so open with Jack. At any time, he could change his mind about her. Anyone could.

"I don't want you to think of me as pathetic," Trudy said with a soft laugh. "I just want you to know that I was done with life back in Boston. I had nowhere to turn and nobody to talk to. I was living for my coffee franchise. But why? They'd become so alien to me. I'd opened too many of them, and I didn't even know any of the people coming in and out of them anymore. Isn't the whole point of opening a coffee shop getting to know your customers? I mean, just in the past three weeks, I've gotten to know the guests at the inn in a totally different way. It's been soul-affirming."

Jack lifted Trudy's hand to his lips and kissed the back of it tenderly. "What do you want to do?" he asked.

Trudy's heart thudded. "I want to run the franchise from here. I have good managers set up at each location, and I can drive down whenever they need me." She rolled her eyes as she remembered: "Of course, every time I've called since I left, they've insinuated that they don't need me at all."

"And we need you here in Wilmington," Jack said, his eyes teasing. "We proved that over and over again. The Festival of Frost Floats never could have happened without you. And the inn! It would have closed! Can you imagine?" He shook his head. "We're pathetic here without you. No pressure, of course." He winked.

Trudy burrowed against his chest and watched the firelight cast its light across the cozy living room, along the hardwood floors and the big bookshelf, laden with so many books she'd never read before. Jack had already told her she could borrow them to her heart's content. "In the spring, I like to go to this spot in the mountains," he'd explained. "Mountain flowers bloom bright and early, a smattering of purples and pinks and yellows. It's a gorgeous place to sit and read."

It felt remarkable to plan so far ahead with someone. Trudy decided to believe in it.

On Christmas morning, Trudy awoke in Jack's arms. Christmas light reflected from the sweeping hills of snow out the back window and still more filtered from a blue sky scattered with clouds. Trudy felt hidden away from the real world.

Jack made them a big pot of coffee and cinnamon rolls drizzled with decadent icing. As they ate, he put a Bing Crosby album in the record player, and it crackled as it started up, drawing them deeper into the Christmas past. As a kid, Trudy's mother had never listened to Christmas music, and she'd learned most of the songs later, surprised that so many were etched into people's cultural consciousness.

Trudy was embarrassed not to take anything to Emily's place for Christmas. "We can't go empty-handed!" she cried as she buttoned her dark green dress to her chin, her wet hair drying in wild curls around her ears.

Jack gazed at her as though she were the most

adorable creature he'd ever seen. "You know what Emily is like. She's not expecting anything. She likes to host!"

But Trudy insisted on stopping at the only store that was open in town, the gas station on the outskirts, where she purchased the most expensive bottle of wine they had on the shelf. It was only twenty-two dollars, and she had a hunch it tasted like garbage.

"This is the first Christmas I've been invited to in years," Trudy told Jack as she stuck the brown bag of wine between her legs in the truck. "I don't want to mess it up. I don't want to seem ungrateful."

"You could never seem ungrateful," Jack assured her, his face stoic. He kissed her again, there in the front of his truck, and her heartbeat quieted. It was going to be all right.

When Jack turned into Emily's driveway, Emily opened the door immediately. She wore a bright red dress with puffy sleeves, and her hair was wild and frizzy from hours of work in the kitchen. Trudy carried the brown bag of wine in one hand and held Jack's in her other, expectation brimming. Inside, "Silver Bells" played on the speaker, and Nina spoke to one of her children, explaining they could have just one cookie each before their big Christmas feast.

Emily wrapped Trudy in a hug there in the warmth of the foyer.

"I brought a very silly gift," Trudy said as their hug broke. She pressed the bag of wine into Emily's arms, and Emily opened it and widened her eyes with laughter.

"Kurt!" Emily called. "Look at this!"

Emily's husband came into the foyer and took the bottle of wine, shaking his head. "Did you tell Trudy about this?"

"I've never told anyone!" Emily said.

"Listen," Trudy interjected, "I know it's a terrible wine. I just couldn't come empty-handed, you know?"

Kurt's eyes danced as he tilted the wine bottle to and fro. "This was the wine Emily and I were drinking when I convinced her to marry me."

Trudy's jaw dropped as Emily's cheeks flashed red at the memory. "You're kidding."

"He's not," Emily said. "We were entirely broke, with fewer than ten dollars in the bank account if you can believe it. I was trying my darndest to work as a chef, throwing myself at every opportunity. Falling in love with someone wasn't in my plan. I'd already avoided it at every turn, you know. Just ask my mother how little I wanted to marry Nina's father."

"Falling in love is never the plan," Trudy offered quietly, drawing her arm around Jack.

"This was the only bottle of wine at this little grocery store near the beach," Emily continued the story. "Kurt bought it and led me out to the water, where he poured us both glasses. I nearly spat it out. It was so terrible."

"Oh no!" Trudy laughed.

"But now, when I drink it, it takes me right back to that night," Emily said wistfully. "It's bizarre how taste can do that, isn't it? It draws you immediately into the memory."

"It's like time travel," Kurt agreed. "Let's all have a glass. Shall we?"

Trudy laughed heartily, amazed at the coincidence. She followed Kurt into the kitchen, where Helen sat with her great-grandchildren, coloring pictures. She was dressed in a beautiful, light-pink dress, and she'd washed, blow-dried, and curled her hair to immaculate, three-dimensional proportions. It was the first Christmas of the rest of her life, and she planned to face it with style.

"Hi, Helen." Trudy bent to hug her.

"Trudy! Hello." Helen reached across the table to collect a framed photograph – the same one of Olivia, Danika, Helen, Brian, and Emily so many years ago. "Look at what Emily got me for Christmas. Aren't I lucky?"

Trudy's heart burst at the image. She would never get over it. "We're all so lucky to be together."

Kurt pressed a glass of the terrible gas station wine into her hand, and Trudy turned toward Jack and draped herself against him. Emily raised her glass toward Kurt, toward her daughter, toward her mother, and finally, toward Trudy, saying, "I'm so glad this winding road of life has led me here with all of you. Merry Christmas."

As Trudy filled her mouth with the tangy wine, she closed her eyes and listened to the bouncing voices around her and filled her nose with the smells of roasted turkey and spiced yams and baking pies. Her heart was so full of emotion she thought she might burst into tears. But when she opened her eyes again, she found Jack before her, gazing at her, his arm wrapped tightly around her to ensure she stayed on solid ground.

# Coming Next in the Series

**Pre Order the Healing of Christmas**

# Other Books by Katie Winters

The Vineyard Sunset Series

Secrets of Mackinac Island Series

Sisters of Edgartown Series

A Katama Bay Series

A Mount Desert Island Series

A Nantucket Sunset Series

The Coleman Series

# Connect with Katie Winters

Amazon
BookBub
Facebook
Newsletter

To receive exclusive updates from Katie Winters please sign up to be on her Newsletter!
CLICK HERE TO SUBSCRIBE

Made in United States
Orlando, FL
02 December 2024

54863705R00115